Twisted Expectations
A Twist in Time Book III

By Brent A. Harris

Based on characters created by Charles Dickens

Twisted Expectation
A Twist in Time Book III

Cover by May Dawney Designs

Copyright © 2024 by Inklings Press

www.inklingspress.com

ISBN: 978-1-7362760-7-5

Dedication:

For my dad,

who was diagnosed with cancer and passed away

during the writing of this book.

You live on through us.

Acknowledgements

I've learned that I cannot do this without my family. When I started writing so long ago, my wife was my first reader while the little ones did their best to keep Daddy from working. My children have since grown and now they're my best helpers. Thanks to Stephanie, Aurora, and Alex for putting up with me and my words and long hours tippity-tapping away on the computer.

I am deeply appreciative of my developmental editor Rob Edwards and my beta readers Jaleta Clegg, Assaph Mehr, and Silvander who provided early feedback, editorial comments, and Britishisms that served to make this book better. Thank you, Jaleta, who also did the fine-tuning proof-copy work. I only wrote the words; it was all of you that made those words make sense.

All errors, historical, anachronistic, grammar-like, or speiling are my own. Any similarities to persons living or dead are likely coincidental, except for you, Ted. I hope you liked being eaten by a dinosaur.

Pip's Prologue

Ours was a land of hardship, a toil upon the marshes as heavy as the fog is bleak, where hope dwells dimly, and great expectations are twisted into despair. The flat landscape, pockmarked by pollards and pockets of brush, stretched limitless beneath the milky air out onto the horizon. Moored in morose waters, a ghostly silhouette of a prison hulk loomed in the distance.

My breath was lost in the misty air of the cold Kent marshlands. I'd stolen out of my sister's place at dawn with a chunk of stale bread. My eye throbbed, and my wrist was swollen and sore. But I had made good on my escape. For it was safe at these times, outside, away from my home. Safe for seven-year-old, Philip Pirrip, Pip for short.

Or rather, the moors had been safe for me – until that fateful time so long ago when a pair of strangers found me in the cemetery.

On the way there, I crept past my uncle's forge, its flame silent in the still morning hour. The forge was to be my future, a fate that I feared. Our pastor once said that lives "were nasty, brutish, and short." I agreed. My life would be no different, the only consolation, if you could call it that, was that I had survived my family's fate.

I reached my parents and five brothers, housed underneath nettles, brambles, and overgrown grasses, each one of them marked with mossy stones. Only my elder sister and I remained. I came here, on occasion, to break bread with the rest of my family in their grave state.

A hand, wet, cold, and slick with slime from the muddy sludge, clasped my shoulder. Shivers shot through my spine. A gravelly voice threatened, "The bread, boy, or your life. Pray I don't take both."

Sharp cold steel pressed against my throat. As beaten and bloodied as I'd been before, I'd never been assaulted with a weapon. No child should. Warm wetness trickled down my trouser leg. At that moment, having already wet myself, I resolved not to let him see me cry.

The rough voice repeated itself. From it, I envisioned someone giant; bald, mustached, and terrible, like some muscleman I'd seen on posters of a passing circus.

"Please, sir," I responded, careful with both my words and my neck. Each movement I made brought with it a fresh bead of blood from the man's blade. I broke a bit of bread off and held it aloft. "If you had but asked, I would have shared. Would you join me?"

"I haven't decided if I should kill you, boy, yet you offer food to me?" I pondered the question and reached a conclusion: crook or not, no one deserves to starve. I gave him both pieces of bread which he accepted greedily once he lowered his blade.

My back was still turned to him, but I could hear his lips smack as he engulfed his prizes. I thought I was safe, that now satisfied, the man would leave me in peace. I was wrong. The knife returned to my throat and my blood went as cold as the blade.

"I think I ought to hoist you upside down, see what other vittles or coin you may have to proffer. I wouldn't want you holding out on me—"

A gunshot erupted across the dawn. Crows clapped their wings and cawed, fleeing for the safety of the skies. I jumped in my skin, startled at the sudden sound. It echoed across the moors.

The criminal's grip went slack. His body was at my heels. Still, I was afraid to move, lest this be some sort of ruse. I didn't understand what was happening, only that I dared not turn around.

"It's all right, lad," a new voice said, gentle and kind. "The danger has passed. Turn around, let me look at you."

I did not look at my rescuer first, I was curious about the man who had attacked me. I was right; thick, balding, but without the mustache I had envisioned. I would have stood no chance against the muscular man. But he was no threat now. His prison garb was soiled by both mud and blood.

"Y-you killed him, sir." My shoulders shuddered. Who was this man with the pistol? Was he a guard from the prison ship, a hero, or a worse villain, perhaps another escaped convict? Was I still in danger?

"One must act decisively. The prisoner was of no consequence, I assure you," the man said. After a long pause, he continued, "but you might be."

I considered the man who had saved me. I wasn't sure I believed him. I found that he possessed a gentle, but sad smile set inside a bushy white beard and mustache. Gold-rimmed glasses sat low on his nose. He wore an earthly-hued suit of browns and a bowler the color of dead grass. To say he looked grandfatherly was as precise of a description that I could give.

The man carried a wound in his stomach, his wrappings were crusted in crimson. His face was layered in age, sweat, and toil. Curly grey hair, disheveled and long, framed his pained state. "Mister," I asked, "are you all right?"

"I need your assistance, lad. Could you tell me where we are? The year?"

"Out on the Marshes of Kent, we are." I gave him the date, or at least what I believed it to be, I wasn't certain of it myself, though I thought the question strange.

"Blast. Too early, too early. I haven't the time left in me." He paced away, his voice trailing, and increasing as he returned. He took the body and dragged it into some bushes behind a crypt out of the watchful eyes of a marble angel. ". . . I've grown old . . . always the wrong time, wrong place . . . no time left. What to do? . . . I need a better plan, one with contingencies, in case I fail."

Afterward he stopped and eyed me the way a tailor might size a suit. I considered the urge to run, but he softened a little. Straightening his hair and patting down his jacket, he regained the poise of a straight-backed gentleman.

"What's your name? Where are your parents?"

"Pip," I answered, pointing behind me to the graves that marked my family. "Stone and bone are all that remain."

"I'm sorry. I know all too well the cruelties and injustices wrought by life." He considered the situation. "So, you were breakfasting with your deceased family when you were attacked?"

I nodded, my fingers tracing the path where the man's blade had been against my throat. The nick had clotted over, but there would be little healing for the memory of this moment, a moment that I would carry forever.

"Walk with me," the man said. It wasn't a question.

"What 'bout him?" I pointed to where the man had dumped the convict's body.

"That's one of the many perks of being a gentleman, Pip," he said walking away from the man he'd just murdered. "The Regulars will be round shortly. The report of my pistol will see to that. They'll come upon the corpse, eventually, long after we're gone, and at the end of the day, this place will hold yet another grave and one less truth. They won't consider suspecting a gentleman from the city out on his own business on the moors."

"A gentleman?" I asked. The man stopped a few feet away. I hadn't decided if I should go with him or run back home. Hopefully my Uncle Joe would be at the forge by now and could help me. Instead, I found my feet following the old man.

"I noticed your eye earlier," he said instead of answering my question. "And your wrist. Those injuries look too settled to be the work of the man who attacked you."

My face fell. "My sister," I answered hesitantly. "She's all that's left. Raised me by hand, as the saying goes."

"Raised by hand, indeed, and a cruel one at that. I'm sorry to hear this, Pip." He shook his head. "Your own hands are already coarse for one so young. What is it that you do?"

"I help my Uncle Joe at the forge. He's been nothing but kind to me, raised me the only way he knows how, as if I were 'is."

"A blacksmith, eh? There's nothing wrong with a profession such as that. But—," he shot me a devilish grin, "is that what *you* want, young Pip?"

My eyes scanned the grey moor, searching through thickets and mud for an answer that I already knew in my heart.

"I want to show you something, something you won't understand yet, but it may change your life. That is, if you agree to help me. But if you do, I'll see you grow into greatness, Pip. Away from all this."

I was curious. And perhaps a bit hopeful. But I was also overwhelmed. My thoughts went to Uncle Joe. Our time at cards. At playing over who could eat our bread and cheese the fastest. The glow he gave to the gloomy greyness. Could I forgo his forge to forge a fate of my own?

We reached an unnatural and rather large pile of brambles and branches. The man set to the task of removing several to reveal a large machine of such a peculiar design that I could not explain it or its purpose. But the effect of seeing such a contraption solidified my thoughts. I had to know everything I could about this gentleman, his machine, and how I could be like him. "Yes," I said eagerly. "I'll help you."

"Excellent," he answered. "Time is short and I hold some rather great expectations, my lad. So, let us begin with haste."

Part I

Chapter 1
The Crystal Palace

Ah, the Crystal Palace. The city's newest monument to itself, built for London's Great Exhibition to showcase the world's leading inventions, innovations, and technology from around the world. Funny how most of its space was reserved exclusively for English exhibits, as if we held a patent on civilization itself. We didn't, of course, but we did a great job convincing ourselves.

So it was with the Crystal Palace and London's Great Exhibition. Light and airy – grandiose. Huge. The Palace resembled an unholy offspring of a train station, a green house, and a cathedral. I'm told, in all, it took over sixty-thousand panes of glass to construct.

It took me about a quarter of an hour to walk the outside length of the Palace, to give you an idea of its size. The glass and cast-iron structure made the attractions and gardens inside all the easier to see – if it weren't for the city's near-perpetual blanket of coal-dark fog. Someone didn't think it through.

But the outlook for today's weather wasn't all bad. In the afternoon, the fog was to take its break for tea and the sun would step in for a few hesitant moments to cover the shift, as if it weren't properly trained for the job and was unsure of what it was supposed to do over London. Shine? Hardly.

The gardens were even grander. It's an hour to circumnavigate labyrinthine paths through the greens and around the central fountain of

Hyde Park. Red brick walkways lined with modern gaslamps wound their way through groves of ivy-coated oak and elm trunks. Tall and ancient trees stood with a history all their own. Out in the open park, statues, fountains, and flowers sprung alive, such was the grandeur of the greens.

Hyde Park was notable for one more thing: it's where Mr. Brownlow's fiancée, Miss Helena Leeford, was murdered just hours before their wedding.

I'm Oliver Twist, aged twenty, and on occasion I've taken on the mantle of *The Orphan.* I try to protect this city and the foundlings just as Mr. Brownlow helped me. He was my mentor, my father-figure, and my friend – until the grief of his loss drove him mad. Thanks to all sorts of peculiar devices I had, including a pocket watch that enabled me to twist the rules of time, Mr. Brownlow was trapped in an alternate London. Forever.

I placed a bouquet of orchids on the grass at the corner of the East Wing. It was the closest spot to her death now that the Palace stood over the actual spot. Mr. Brownlow once told me orchids were her favorite. She would have liked these – fully bloomed and pale lavender, like the ribbons she wore. And Brownlow, in turn, would have liked to have known that I tried to keep the memory of them both alive.

I placed flowers every time I came to Hyde Park. Usually, I walked here for exercise or to think about my current case, or to clear my mind. Today, I was on business. I was here to hear a proposal.

Of course, that meant I had to go inside the Palace, a visit I'd avoided until now. It was one thing to be among the crowds on the open greens surrounding the Exhibition Hall. It was quite another to be crammed inside like sardines – no, sardines came in a can – like too small a goldfish bowl filled with a frenzy of fish during feeding time.

On the inside, through the throngs of visitors at the over 14,000 exhibits, adding in stops for food and breaks at the newly designed loo, the Crystal Palace was a crowded, smelly, all-day affair. But I wasn't to be among the muddled masses.

No, I was heading to the upper echelons, the higher chamber of the Crystal Palace, among the catwalks and cafes where the London Elite had little time to waste on such pedestrian bores as crowds and queues. Up there, in the airy glass building, elevated above the fray, was little place for an orphan like me. But, you see, I'd been invited.

I was ushered in through the VIP entrance – no wait there - and hustled up the wrought-iron staircase into high society like a sinner on his way to heaven.

But, perhaps, this was all a well-earned reward? I had saved the city at least once or twice. I was earning a reputation. Whether it was good or bad, no one bothered to say. Maybe my newfound friend would tell me.

"Twist." The voice rang out above the din of the crowded convention center. It sounded as if I had just been caught swiping a kerchief and all of Fleet Street had witnessed it, pointed a finger at me, and glared disapprovingly. Of course, that could simply be my own insecurities, being a former thief and street robin, after all.

"So glad you could make it," the voice said again. He introduced himself as Philip Pirrup, "but call me, Pip."

He was roughly my height, my age, and held the same look in his eyes as mine that spoke of a childhood better left unspoken. Pip pumped my hand hard before letting go. I had to shake it off. Two others stood from their seats, one I knew and the other I did not.

The trio were all dressed in what would pass as most people's Sunday best – except it was a Saturday. Pip had on an indigo waistcoat, a puffy silk vest and a Puff Tie wrapped around a stiff high collar like a snake around a mouse. He had to have been insufferably warm under the glass roof but gave no indication of discomfort. His friend looked the same, but in a more boring brown. And the gentleman that I knew and who had arranged today's affair, wore his typical, but orderly and crisp Peeler's uniform with copper buttons. Even still, they all gave off the appearance that they were dressed down.

I, however, had on my best attire, wearing black (as one does when moonlighting as a vigilante) with nothing so formal around my neck but a plain cream cravat, and a decidedly yellowed white shirt, as if I had scheduled church at noon and a pauper's funeral at one. I was, by wardrobe alone, outmatched.

"You are most welcome here," Pip said, as if intruding on my thoughts. "You are an inspiration, a hero, and an all-around solid chap from what I've heard."

I let a particular word linger around for a moment. *Welcomed.* How had Pip known what I've sought my entire life? He must have known how difficult it was to be cast aside, orphaned and alone with no parent to look up to, no one to help navigate an indifferent world. I saw in him the same struggles I knew. Yet, he had made it. He had found his place. Why couldn't I?

Or had I? Was this the beginning of it?

I didn't realize my hunger until this moment. I wanted to gorge myself. Not because I sought wealth but because I was so tired. Tired of struggling. Tired of scrounging for food week after week. Tired of struggling to find a family, only to be betrayed by the man who took me in. And finally, I was tired of struggling to keep the foundlings who were under my care clothed, fed, and warm in this unforgiving city.

Another word Pip had spoken circled my mind. *Hero.* Yes, perhaps I was. After all, I'd saved this city twice. Once, from Mr. Brownlow's attempt at destroying the Strand. Then, there was the matter of Mr. Scrooge and his spirits . . . and of Nell.

I missed her. She was another casualty, someone else I couldn't save. I needed—

"Love," Pip's voice said, the word shaking me loose from my thoughts.

"I'm sorry, what was that?" I asked.

"Please, we'd love to have you join us," Pip repeated. "Have a seat." Pip had a higher-pitched voice, like a parrot, that cut across the din. But Pip also possessed a charismatic quality. It was . . . welcoming. I was being welcomed into this fold, creases and all.

Inspector Bucket motioned over to a chair currently occupied, but its owner, a bookish young man sitting alone, magically vacated it for me. I nervously took over the chair that was still warm. Talk about a hot seat. I placed my crystal-lensed goggles and my hat onto my oversized cane and leaned them against the table as close to me as possible as I observed what the others had done.

I eyed Bucket warily. As an Inspector, he was sharp and cunning, a great detective. It didn't help that he knew who I was, and he could arrest me on the spot. Vigilantism wasn't tolerated by Scotland Yard. Yet, he made no such move. And I had no idea why.

The man in brown introduced himself as Herbert Pocket, and by all appearances, his were deep, as he ordered for our table a presumably expensive bottle of champagne. We sat at a feast of oysters, salmon, fruits, and small cakes.

"Ah, Mr. Twist, help yourself, have an oyster, last month of the year in season." Pip pushed the platter toward me.

I didn't know oysters had seasons, or how to eat one, but they were all staring at me expectantly, so I took one and gave it a go with a knife, prising a piece of the slippery meat out from its shell and shoving it into my mouth with the blade.

Pip laughed, but it was in such an oh-so-polite way that I couldn't possibly take offense from it. "Oh no dear, boy, oysters are a tricky thing."

He took his knife, loosened the insides, squirted some lemon juice over it, slurped the thing down whole, all while I was still chewing mine. I gulped mine down, as the slimy critter forced my lips and tongue to contort like an acrobat. I stifled a gag, a practiced reflex from years of eating moldy bread and cheese. The others seemed bemused by my ignorance, but not malicious. Still, I started sweating under my collar, like I was a fish at an interview for a job climbing trees.

Speaking of fish, something smelled of it here, and it wasn't the seafood on the table. Why had Pip invited me here? What was his plan? I'd been in this position before, with Brownlow and Scrooge at his steam-works. Pip wouldn't be the first to ask of me what I couldn't – or wouldn't – do.

"I'll skip these, thank you." I also ignored the smoked salmon and made for a small strawberry sponge cake with cream, food I knew I could eat with some measure of confidence. Where was a minced pie when you needed one?

"I'm glad you accepted my invitation," Pip said after slurping down another oyster, "I've a proposal that might interest you."

My ears perked. I'd met a version of Pip in a previous adventure, so it tugged at my curiosity when I found out that *a* Pip did live in London and furthermore, he was interested in meeting me. I had accepted this Pip's invitation, which included a VIP tour of the Palace, with a certain interest.

"Do tell," I prodded.

"They say a man in possession of a fortune must be in want of a wife," Herbert Pocket said. I picked up some subtle sarcasm in his voice in a phrase that rang familiar to me, but I couldn't place it.

"But that's not true at all," Pip explained, as Pocket's champagne was poured all around. "They merely want more fortune."

Pocket burst with laughter as he and Pip raised their glasses. Bucket joined in, as the realization hit me that Pocket and Bucket would make a good name for a comedy duo. Since I didn't understand their joke, my own helped me blend in with the others during his toast to, 'the finer things in life.'

"You see, Mr. Twist," Pip went on after settling his glass on the table.

"Call me Oliver, please." I turned my spoon toward my dessert, London social conventions be damned.

"Ah, well, certainly, uh . . . Oliver." Pip picked up a spoon. It was tinier than the one I held. "You'll want a custard spoon, I imagine, and also, it's customary to hold it underhand, ol' chap." He said it with such a smile that I almost didn't notice us swapping spoons. I was more curious than offended. *Different utensils?* I was learning a lot in just a few minutes' conversation. I couldn't help but think Pip's corrections came from a place of sincerity. But it reminded me of just how much of a round peg I was in a room fit for squares. With some rigorous sanding, could I be made to fit here too? Did I even want that?

I think I did.

"I need you, Oliver." Pip said matter-of-factly.

It was nice to be needed. "How so?"

"I'm making a run for Parliament. I've already secured Bucket's blessing." With that, Bucket raised a glass, not the champagne but a beer, and drained it.

"Pip here will make a fine MP," he said, after a moment of beating down his chest to circumvent a beer burp. I never understood the allure of liquor. I've had my fair share of it, but it was mostly to help keep warm on cold nights. Under the glass of the Crystal Palace, it was already plenty warm.

Okay, so Parliament Pip, sure. But that still didn't answer why I was here. Or why Bucket hadn't arrested me on the spot.

Pip corrected the placement of my napkin on the table and informed me, with a smile, that it belonged in one's lap. I'd not had much use for napkins. That's what sleeves were for.

I don't remember much from what Mr. Brownlow tried to teach me about etiquette and such. I never saw myself as a gentleman, therefore the lessons never stuck. Maybe it was time for me to learn, starting with napkins. But, if I couldn't remember something simple like proper napkin placement, then it made me wonder why Pip needed me.

"Bucket secures my vote with those who want tougher laws and more police presence on the street," Pip said.

"And the other side?" Things were starting to click into place.

"Yes, the reformers, those who want a more, let's say, delicate touch."

I knew firsthand what you were capable of when gnawing hunger ate at you. I'd stolen to eat. So, as the Orphan, I'd been known not just to stop criminals, but to also feed and shelter them. One such fellow ran my soup kitchen. Not all criminals were bad people – some had suffered bad breaks.

"Rubbish," Bucket said. "A tiger doesn't become less dangerous because you feed it. It just associates the hand with food. Sooner or later, it'll bite it off."

"Be that as it may," Pocket interjected, "Pip wants to secure his seat, and to do that, he'll have to win the reformers too."

"Quite right," Pip said. "Compromise shouldn't be a dirty word. And that's where you come in, Oliver. I propose a partnership."

I dropped the tiny dessert spoon.

"We'll get you a nice set of clothes." He nodded politely at my rags. I happened to like them, they were well worn and comfortable. But I understood his point. He continued, "and whatever gadgets and gizmos you need for your vigilantism."

So, that's why Bucket hadn't hauled me off to the Yard. We were on the same team now. Even so, Bucket's big brown eyes narrowed intensely. I don't think he liked me. Maybe if he approached criminals as people instead of problems, we'd become better mates. Also, I liked gadgets and gizmos. They'd gotten me out of many tight situations. Of course, no one could replace Nell, not even—

"That's dodging the point," Pip continued, "More importantly, we'll also provide you funding for your shelter. For the next year."

That part landed. I would have dropped a second spoon if I could have. Most of my money, inherited from Brownlow, had been sunk into rebuilding the Curiosity Shop, and its neighboring soup kitchen. The problem with charity is that it didn't turn a profit, a fact that scared off investors.

I resisted the urge to accept right there. I knew better, and I needed time to think. There was always a catch to these sorts of things. Good people didn't appear out of nowhere, flush with cash. But Pip *had* appeared in London seemingly out of thin air with his pockets full. What was his story?

I had to know.

Chapter 2
Pip's Past

"I'll consider your offer," I told him.

Pip had locks of black hair which he smoothed back when he was about to speak. "I wouldn't dream of imposing. Take all the time you need. Let's chat, get to know each other."

Pocket piped up, "I'm curious to see the exhibit of extinct creatures they have here. It'll be a good time for us to all talk as we tour."

As much as I looked forward to exploring, bones sounded rather boring. I liked technology, the future, not the past. I spent enough time reliving that as it was.

"But before we take the tour, why don't I tell you a little bit about me." Pip leaned back in his chair, his posture loosening for perhaps the first time since we'd met. "The problem is, I hate talking about myself, I know you'll understand."

Yes, I knew the feeling, but mine was born of being told I didn't matter. Was this what it felt like to be an imposter? I wasn't sure. But I sure had the feeling that Pip liked to hear others talk about him. If his head grew any larger, I might have to pop it like an airship's balloon.

Without missing his cue, Pocket spoke up to sing Pip's praises. "He's a wunderkind, always knew just what investments to make, which to back off, as if he were a modern-day Merlin or a possessed an uncanny knowledge of the future."

If I'd been drinking, I would have spit it out. Instead, I beckoned the blood in my face to beat a hasty retreat, lest I give anything away. Knowledge of the future? Hmmm. Interesting choice of words. I wondered why Pocket would choose them.

Perhaps it was a happy coincidence. I hoped my skin would return to its normal pallor before anyone noticed that I'd flushed red and given myself away. They knew that I was the Orphan, but did they also suspect that I traveled through time?

I sensed that Bucket was suspicious. Maybe that's why he reluctantly agreed to my presence. I'd solved a few cases, even he couldn't deny that I might be of some aid. Maybe I was Bucket's bloodhound, here to sniff the truth out. Or maybe I was just bait.

"No one backed steam-power. Especially with the unfortunate business of Mr. Brownlow," Pocket continued. "But Pip did. He invested heavily. Steam-power is in our homes now. In the skies. Soon to be in our streets with steam-cycles and horseless carriages. As a result, Pip has walked away with a fortune."

Steam-cycles were my fault. Dodger had built me one. It was certainly rudimentary, but now that the concept was out, well, more people wanted one. Should Dodger somehow desire it, she'd do well in any mechanical pursuit. Just don't try to replace Nell.

Bucket coughed. Apparently, it was his turn to sing. "That would be impressive enough if it were his only investment that's paid dividends. But no, somehow, he's backed railroads, textile factories, copper guilds, and they've all flourished, with nary a misstep." After a bit of a ribbing chuckle, Bucket continued, "of course, there was that one instance—"

"If you're referring to that wager at Wimbeldon," Pip explained, "I had been enjoying a fine French Bordeaux, with a wonderful hint of gooseberry, so I was hardly in the right frame of mind—"

"Maybe you're a time-traveler?" I interrupted. But unlike Pocket's ambiguity, I meant it. Despite my earlier attempts at hiding my surprise, I determined that I wanted to get his gut reaction. Though it was improbable, in my line of work with spirits and magical watches and who knew what else, I had to discover if there was another person out there who could bend the rules of time. *Nell would have known.*

"I appreciate your jest, Oliver." Pip gave me nothing. Note to self: don't play at Knaves with him. "But as a fellow orphan, you know where we whetted our wits. They're praising me more than I deserve I should think."

Pip presented a disarming smile. That must have worked well with potential partners, business and romantic alike.

"I see," I said.

He went on: "I was lucky at first, but as luck turned me from a black smith's apprentice to a prim and proper gentleman, I forged my learnings and experience as a boy into who I am now. I learned very quickly that time is short. I could have died long ago, been buried along with my family. The clock doesn't owe you a second. You have to take what you want, and you have to do it *now.*"

"Reap the benefits of boldness." Bucket nodded his head approvingly. "I know what you mean."

"We are all gamblers on this Earth. And there's no such thing as grey on a roulette wheel, is there?" Pip asked. "Go all in. Red or black. Because one day, that roulette wheel stops spinning, and a color is called."

With my luck, it'd land on the green zero. But I knew what Pip meant. If I had been tasked with sniffing out the scent of the situation by Bucket, he would be seriously disappointed in me. I could smell nothing afoul. Pip simply possessed intelligence and insight that served him well, mixed with a tenacity of taking bold risks. Attributes likely gathered from survival on the streets. Necessity. After all, when you had nothing to lose, risk was a net positive.

I was beginning to understand Pip. He and I seemed similar, there was an air of familiarity with him, with notable differences, as if we weren't necessarily on the same page, but different books on the same shelf.

I had gone through a similar life story, though not to the degree Pip had. I'd been self-taught, read Brownlow's books, had pulled myself out of near starvation (with some help, of course). Pip had done it in spades.

He'd suffered as much as I but had come out on the other end a gentleman. Pip earned it. As he straightened his waistcoat and his spine to lean in from his seat, I realized his hard-won station suited him.

I wondered why I lacked the ability to move up in life. Perhaps it was because Brownlow had taken me in. Maybe he'd made me too soft and reliant. Or perhaps the fact that Brownlow and I had met *was* the result of a gamble. I could have run away. I could have robbed him. He thought I had, for a time. But he became the best thing to happen to me – at least until he turned into a villain. Maybe my intuition wasn't all that great.

My thoughts turned to Dodger. I wondered what she would have made of all this. And I wondered, not for the first time, why she still lived the way she did, one roll of the dice at a time, never quite knowing what number it was. She was talented, smart, and cunning. Couldn't she have chosen to better herself and her station by now? Didn't she possess all the brains and tenacity of Pip? Or, perhaps like many people, she'd placed it all onto black and life had come up red.

I lowered my head, as if in mourning. If life was a gamble, it was one where the house always won in the end. If I had any chance of improving my odds, I'd need to learn what I could from those around this table. I had much to think about regarding Pip's proposal, but I found myself leaning into it.

"Come, Oliver, it's time for the tour." Pip stood, so Pocket and Bucket did the same. I pushed away my plate, scooted back the cast iron chair, and wondered where I should place my cloth napkin. I decided on the chair before I realized everyone else had put theirs on their plates. Hadn't he said not to put it on the table?

It was too late to fix my mistake as my hands were now full, having retrieved my belongings. Pip placed his hand on my shoulder, guiding me along the upstairs catwalk where our canes clattered, high above the crowds below. Where we passed people on our level, they parted like the Red Sea for us. This was Pip's party; everyone else was simply a guest.

"Pocket and I want to show you an exhibit here I know you'll find awe-inspiring," Pip said. There was excitement in his eyes, as if he were a child again. His pace quickened and his neck craned for a better view through the crowd to the exhibition hall below. "These new exhibits are all the rage. Scientists have uncovered animals from our distant past. Creatures called dinosaurs."

Chapter 3
Ooohing and Aaahing

According to the papers, ten years ago, biologist Richard Owen first uttered the name *dinosaur,* ushering in a whole new era of scientific research. Names have power. With that power, he breathed life into the dust of the Earth, resurrecting long extinct creatures. He captivated the minds and hearts of children and adults alike. Owen, and others of his ilk, excited our imaginations with terrible and great creatures. I confess, I was intrigued.

In ten short years, the discovery of the dinosaurs shook our faith in our place as rulers of the Earth. We were faced with uncomfortable questions: How could anything get so big? What was their life like? But more importantly: what happened to them? How could creatures so large and terrifying disappear off the face of the Earth? And what did that mean for us?

Dinosaurs proved that life was fleeting. Nothing, not even gigantic beasts could withstand the tests of time. For time was the enemy of all creatures, great and small.

Their mystery had become somewhat a fixture in our culture, such was their thrall. From the steam-powered displays in the Crystal Palace, to the dinosaur sculptures outside (which I had been told was next on our tour) to the many books and articles written, you couldn't go a day without hearing of some new discovery, story, or statue.

Even the popular Dickens himself had written about a Megalosaurus mucking about in bleak London mud and fog. My own experience with his fabrication of my life's story colored my opinion of the wily writer. But, after seeing the creatures for the first time in my life, spread out in the hall below, I felt safe in saying that Dickens did not do the dinosaur justice.

We had managed some distance from the crowded café to the VIP catwalks above the dinosaur displays. I caught my first glimpse of the bones and my whole body froze in place, my hands gripped the iron railing, becoming one. The skeletons were bigger than I imagined, more majestic, and if I'm being honest, more terrifying.

Pip and Pocket skirted around me. Bucket had seemed more interested in the crowd, scanning it with a policeman's eyes, but even he kept drawing back to the beasts below. Even as bones, they rose majestically into the air of the Palace, heads high above the crowd, and only a handful of feet under ours.

There were three skeletons, no, four. I didn't know the names of any of them but seeing them there made me want to know their story and everything about them. I looked to Pip for answers.

"Impressive, aren't they?" he said, his voice bubbling.

"I could stand here all day."

"Apologies, I had arranged a private tour with Richard Owen himself, but I found the man quite disagreeable. However, I've read his work and heard his lectures, so we'll muddle through, though I admit I'm a poor substitute."

"Owen?" I asked incredulously. I knew the name, but I was impressed that Pip knew him personally. However, the squeaked-out way I had spoken it aloud sounded as if I were ignorant of the man. In this company, I might as well have been.

"Yes, the biologist," Pip answered politely, as if I'd had a lapse of memory instead of a lack of breeding. "Let's begin, shall we?"

There were placards attached to the railings to let us know which creatures were which, but Pip told us instead, as if he possessed the entirety of the *Encyclopedia Britannica* in his head. "Dinosaur bones have been discovered throughout time," he began. "Yet, no one really knew what they were. The bones of giants?"

"Or dragon teeth," Bucket scoffed. "Of course, we know better, now."

"Quite right. It wasn't until recently that biologists discovered that they belonged to a whole order of extinct creatures."

The comedy duo nodded in agreement. But I couldn't help consider that if dinosaurs could exist, why couldn't a dragon? In truth, I could see a dinosaur with leathery wings beating above my head. The thought made me glad that I was standing here above their remains instead of below an actual, alive creature.

"But in those following years," Pip donned a tour guide's amplified voice, "our knowledge of the creatures has flourished, thanks to our enlightenment, intelligence, and perseverance at uncovering and digging out these ancient mysteries."

What I learned from dinosaurs came from newspapers and Pip. He was a font of knowledge. It made sense, as these dinosaurs were new and indeed all the rage, and of course Pip seemed to be on the cusp of every trend. He seemed to bask in both the warming glass building and his own knowledge, like a lizard on a rock. Like a dinosaur? Were dinosaurs lizards?

The catwalk continued in a giant rectangle that circuited this wing of the Crystal Palace, overlooking the dinosaurs and other exhibits. After moving past the more generalized signs that taught us about dinosaurs, we made it to the first display. My heart raced as I stretched my neck to see it. I caught I glimpse of a smaller creature (compared to its kin), its bones browned, its skeleton posed victoriously, for it had been resurrected, in a way. But what was it?

"Here we have an Hylaeosaurus," Pip said, pronouncing it again as, "Hi-lee-o-saur-us." It was hard to hear among the shouted echoes of, "ooohs," and "aaahs," from below. Oh, wait, some of those were my own.

It was a squabby little armored thing, except it wasn't little. Like a fat frog the size of a carriage who had a child with a tortoise. Children pointed fingers at it with smiles smacked on their faces.

And then it moved.

Were they supposed to move?

Sometime between my heart lurching into my throat and settling back down, Pip explained. "That's right. These skeletons are not static. They move, as scientists thought they might, through the ingenuity of science and steam-power."

As we continued our tour, I realized that among the chaos of the crowds, each of the dinosaurs was moving.

"There are gears between sections of spine, at the hips, and neck and jaws, which serve to articulate the creatures," Pip lectured. "Pistons move feet up and down. The Hyleasoraus can pivot its head and swish its tail as its feet move."

It could have been creepy, as if the dinosaurs belonged as decorations to a macabre masquerade ball. But in the context of the exhibit hall, as children and adults learned about them, the jerky movements of the skeletons made them more real, even more alive. If you slapped some muscles and skin on them, they could stomp right on out of here.

"There are phonographs playing recordings of a tropical jungle and approximate noises of what each dinosaur may have sounded like, though we can hardly hear it over the crowds. Dreadfully sorry," Pip apologized. Now that I knew what to listen for, I could make out the faint rumblings and effects interspersed in the background, with no way to tell which sounds belonged to what. Still, it added to the idea that you'd travelled way back in time. I briefly wondered if I could convince my pocket watch to send me back to the age of the dinosaurs. Probably a bad idea.

"This is an Iguanodon." Pip broke into my thoughts as we examined the next display. Again, he said the creature's name more slowly, "e-gwa-na-don, for iguana tooth."

It did resemble an oversized lizard, right down to the scales I was imagining. The dinosaur had a lone horn, about the size of a thumb, on its nose. I watched as it rose up on its hind legs, its fore legs braced against a palm tree, while its skeletal teeth attempted to eat a frond dangling just out of reach.

We wasted no time moving on as the next display was hard to miss. In the center of the room, with a head held high like a giraffe's, stood the largest creature.

"Camarasaurus," Pip explained, though it sounded like he said 'camera' to me, "a sauropod." No matter where we were on the catwalk, the incredible behemoth could be seen from every angle. Its long tail whipped over the heads of the crowd. Any lower and this would instead be a reenactment of the French Revolution. Anyways, 'sauropod' must have been Latin for "BIG." I think it was my favorite dinosaur so far.

But it was short-lived.

"Here we come to the apex predator." Pip pointed below to a fearsome creature. "The mighty Megalosaurus."

I shuddered, even though I was quite safe. It was involuntary, perhaps a warning embedded into us by our ancient ancestors to warn of danger, even if that danger had been dead for long, long time.

I could understand why. With teeth the size of small shears and as sharp too, I didn't want to be anywhere near it. Gears gnashed its crocodile-like jaw closed as if it were taking bites out of its audience. I noticed that most of the children stood behind their parents, though there were a few fearless ones pressed right up against the edge of the display.

"The exhibitors have this girl mounted on all fours. I don't think that's quite right, I believe she may have stood bipedally." Pip looked at me, and I couldn't help but be insulted when he explained, "upright." But before I could defend my education (or lack thereof) the idea of a Megalosaurus, towering over me, taller than the gates of Buckingham Palace, scared away any offense. And everything else.

"And that concludes the tour of the fossils." Pip said. Pocket and Bucket looked like a couple of kids locked in a sweets store overnight. If I could see myself, I probably looked the same. I could feel the excitement flow through my veins like a runaway locomotive. Pip continued, "It's amazing how exquisite and rare these rocks are."

"Rocks? I presumed that these were the dinosaurs' own bones, are they not?" The question came from Bucket, who looked confused. I was too as I had the same thought but didn't want to ask. What are fossils and why did he call them rocks?

"Technically, nothing you see here are bones. They are the calcified mineral impressions left behind in a process called lithification, which transforms bones into—" Pip stopped and held out both hands, as if waving himself down off a soapbox. "Apologies, chaps, I have a habit of bursting into trivia."

That was all right with me. I was happy to learn from him, happy to be here, and exhilarated to have seen these dinosaurs. I wanted more.

"We have the entirety of the Palace to tour, including the arboretum and a whole other wing," Pip guided us to a roped off staircase that descended to the first floor and a set of doors. "But I thought it best to continue our exploration of the extinct to keep on theme. We're now going to take a stroll through the greens of the Benjamin Hawkins Waterford sculptures, including his dinosaurs. He recreated an Iguanodon so large, that he hosted a dinner party for twenty people inside it, which I was invited to attend."

Of course he was.

"Let's take a stroll out onto the grounds and see what these bygone beasts would have really looked like, shall we gentlemen?"

I also wanted to see the newest inventions exhibited here. A man by the name of Babbage had apparently upgraded his steam-powered difference-engine and built it into a mechanical contraption, a machine he called a robot. I was told that not only could it act as a sort of math tool, but that it could also perform basic tasks. It was a curious thing, but my visit there had become overshadowed by my desire for dinosaurs and my pleasant company. So, the difference-engine made into machine would have to wait.

I was getting to know the mysterious young Pip and starting to understand him. And I was beginning to like what I saw. He was a charismatic social climber with ambition oozing from his pockets and buckets. I couldn't help but to be swept up in his enthusiasm. I think I was beginning to make fast friends.

Our group took the stairs out into the gardens on the other side of the Palace from where I had entered. The sun, despite its efforts to greet us warmly, left us cooler than we had been inside. Sweat condensed around my neck. And a breeze brought to me an unexpected chill.

Chapter 4
Do You Think She Saurus?

There were two things I noted when we left the Palace. A statue of a mean-looking Megalosaurus that made the skeleton inside look like a puppy, and an old friend, slinking in the shadows. I ignored her and followed Pip over to the dinosaur.

The courtyard opened to a labyrinth of hedges, pebbled paths, unlit gaslamps, and oaks. Only, in this maze, it was not a minotaur but other monsters lurking in the bushes. As we traversed the wide path, it narrowed and split in a myriad of directions. Some headed into a grove of elms, while others diverged to different gardens of Hyde Park. Pip led us through lollygagging crowds closer to the carnivorous beast.

The cement and brick statue sat among fern-like shrubs, staring us down and sizing us up. It was – like its skeletal cousin inside – squatting on all fours.

"Should be standing on two," Pip reminded us. I could almost make out drool on its sharp, curved teeth. Perhaps it missed having food in its stomach, maybe it was jealous of the dinner party hosted inside the belly of the Iguanodon. All I knew was, I wouldn't want to meet one in real-life.

Behind the statue, a verdant hill rose, obstructing our view further on. More elms and oaks surrounded us, their shadows enclosed us, trapping us with this bygone beast. Fortunately, the shadow of another familiar figure had, uh, shadowed me, giving me an excuse to seek some air.

I patted down the lining of my coat to check and make sure my pocketbook was there. It was. So, she wasn't here to rob me, in which case, I never would have noticed her. That must mean she wanted to talk. Or she was slipping and getting soft. I chuckled inwardly at the thought.

Dodger.

She only made herself known when she wanted to be seen. Otherwise, she was a ghost. Well, not a literal ghost, like Nell had been. Ever since the awkward but comforting moment between us on the frozen lake, things had been strained, as if neither knew our next words. It was the way she had nestled her head on my shoulder, the way I'd wrapped my arm around her. Pity we hadn't talked to each other much since, I might have figured out what it all meant.

Usually, Dodger wanted me dead. But not lately. We seemed to have moved past that to a stage more *uncertain*. Maybe I could ask her? I chuckled in my head again.

Anyway, I was in esteemed company and Dodger was there all dirty, disheveled, and, well, Dodger-y. I wasn't sure I wanted her sticking around and having them spot her with me. It would take a lot of explaining to the Chief of Police and the polished and proper Pip and Pocket what I was doing consorting with someone of her social status. To them, she was a common criminal even if there was nothing common about her.

"Excuse me, Pip, Pocket, Bucket," I said politely. "You all go on ahead, I need to make use of the, uh water-closet. I'll find you."

"Are you sure it's not because of our friend here?" Pip chided, pointing to the creature. But there was a tone to his voice, a tone that told me he knew I was lying. He saw through me like one could see through the walls of the Crystal Palace. "We'll meet you by the Iguanodons."

"Don't get eaten by anything while you're gone." Pocket pointed to the Megalosaurus too.

"They'd spit me out. I'm not tasty," I said taking my leave to the toilets. I made my way down a quieter path ducking behind a grove of trees out of sight of the others and waited for her to show.

***

"What are you doing here?" I gave Dodger the once over: a light coat, black with copper buttons obviously purloined from finer threads, hastily sewn on. A new top hat with freshly polished goggles (likely pilfered) and a crooked smile that locked away more secrets than the Tower of London.

"Same thing as you are." She brushed a strand of dark hair aside. "I've got Abbey and the others with me. Apparently, the younger you are, the easier it is to say '*Iguanodon.*' They're all eating it up in there like butter on bacon."

I nodded in thanks. Dodger had been spending more time with the foundlings, all the while dodging any real conversation with me. It's like she wanted to express herself but didn't know how. I knew that feeling.

"Wait, how'd you get in?" the question occurred to me. Wait, I knew the answer. "You know I could have gotten you tickets, you didn't have to sneak them all in."

"Tickets and queues, where's the fun in that?" she winked.

The air between us felt heavier than all the anchors of the *H.M.S. Waterloo.* I broke the silence by noticing that she was up to her old tricks again. "Dodger, there's a red silk handkerchief sticking out of your pocket."

"No harm getting some honest work in. Nothing they wouldn't miss. These rich blokes casually forget or drop belongings that would mean meals for the rest of us."

My esteemed company came to mind. What if they saw us together? Bucket was likely to hang her on the spot. And Pip, well, what would he think? With as much contraband as Dodger was carrying, it might be a good idea that no one saw us together. I stepped back, perhaps a bit too obviously.

"Don't want your new high-class friends seeing you with the uncouth and street-savvy Dodger? That's right, I saw you colluding with them up on high. I guess I'm too low for you?"

She shrank back, like a wounded sparrow. I moved in closer, but it was already too late for apologies. I caught wind of the street smells she'd brought with her from horse dung to a breath of gin. The sourness teared my eyes. Perhaps some distance was best.

"You mean, because you're a thief?" I asked. Her pockets were bulging.

"Not my fault that I find things." She cocked her hat crookedly.

"Usually those 'things' are still attached to the people you relieve them from."

She shrugged off the dig. "I never said where I found them." We were far enough away from the others that we decided to walk openly, with the space between us naturally disappearing, along the hill beside the Crystal Palace. It was less busy here, with the open space and sprawling picnic areas dispersing the heavy crowds.

I knew I should meet back with the others soon, but this was the longest moment alone with Dodger I'd had since the time on the ice after we'd lost Nell.

Dodger was missing her too, even if she grieved differently than I. My sleeve carried my mourning. Her distance carried hers. That distance also carried with it the unspoken words between us. Words I wasn't sure I wanted to hear now. Not with the mysterious Pip pulling at my brain. With the cooling winds at my back and Dodger near my side, I struggled between wanting to remove my coat to wanting to pull it on tighter.

"So, who are they?" she asked. There was jealousy in her voice, but also a vulnerability that I rarely heard from her. "I mean, other than the overgrown Peeler."

"Pip and Pocket," I answered. The names sounded absurd when spoken aloud.

"Pocket, huh?" she snorted. "And Pip? What, as in pipsqueak? Like the last one?" Right. I must have told her about the Pip from a different timeline.

"Just Pip," I said. We continued walking. "He wants to fund us, and the kitchen too. He wants a partnership as he runs for office. I can't pass up that offer."

"Throwing money around?" Dodger considered her words for a moment. She was always quick on the comebacks, silence meant thought. "Sounds like Pip wants to be a hero without doing the hard work. Making hard choices. Don't take it, something's not right."

I thought I had still been mulling it over. In truth, I had made my decision. Dodger was wrong.

"Don't get tempted by your newfound friends Oliver," she warned. "I drink gin from a bottle, and you think me uncouth. They sip it from a fancy glass with some gross green olives thrown in and suddenly that makes it fancy?"

Obviously, Dodger could see the difference, couldn't she? "I've been invited to join them. Maybe I should, maybe our efforts at improving London would be more successful with them?"

Ahead, statues of twin Iguanodons stood over us. They were massive things, one asleep and the other on guard against threats. Absently, we'd been walking right toward them. Pip could see us together at any moment—

"You've gone daft if you think any of that is true. You have a habit of making dangerous new allies," Dodger said. And she knew a thing or two about that, having killed me at least once. But now look at us, best of mates.

"Well, then, perhaps it's better that I stick close by Pip, and uncover the truth?" There was bitterness in her voice, so I returned it with some annoyance in mine. Couldn't Dodger see what I was doing? Besides, maybe Pip was as harmless as a garter snake. "You're wrong about him."

She shook her head. "Stay far away. Like a steam-pipe burst, Oliver. The closer you are the worse the burn."

"Look I can't be talking to you now." I looked over my shoulder for Pip.

"I don't like it, Oliver. It's not you, one bit. You're playing a dangerous game. I've dodged the noose more times than is fair, yet somehow, I keep on living. Soon enough though, even my time will come, it always does," Dodger warned before going silent. She was being thoughtful again. I gave her the time to collect her words before she continued, "What matters is the company you keep, the people you choose to spend that short time in between the pram and the hangman." Her voiced cracked and quieted but I thought I heard her say, "it matters who you lo—"

"There you are, ol' boy," Pip said excitedly. "Thought you'd gotten lost. There's a commotion over by the Megalosaurus statue – where we just were – that I think we need to investigate. He nodded reluctantly at my companion. "Who's your, uh friend?"

Dodger didn't move or speak. Vulnerable and frozen, the two words least likely to define her. Dodger's lost words, Pip's frantic intrusion, I needed a moment to process but there was no time, like a steam-engine barreling ahead, about to derail.

"Uh, this is . . ." I stumbled.

"Dodger," she offered a grimy hand, which Pip took. "Pleased to meet you, Guv'nor."

"Yes, she's my uh . . . contact," I continued, through Dodger's glare. "I mean to say, she's—"

"You don't need to explain, you probably have connections with all walks of society." Pip subtly wiped his hand down with a fine silk kerchief (chances are he wouldn't see that again). "I see the need to associate yourself with the sort."

"Hey, sort yourself, mate, I'm pleased to be nothing like you." She drew close enough to Pip to make the man uncomfortable. "You and your fancy coat and shiny gears and buttons." Dodger touched them all, ruffling the man's clothes (and there went the kerchief). My face flushed. This was exactly why I didn't want Pip to meet her. "Dodger."

She continued to play with Pip's accoutrements, this time pulling on the leather band of his goggles affixed to his top hat. "Dodger," I said, more sternly this time. "Give Pip back his pocketbook and kerchief. Please."

Dodger swirled, happy with herself, fetching a fat pocketbook from her coat and handing it back over to its rightful owner. "Just having a spot o' fun."

Pip, for his part, played it off, much to my relief. "Well, that was delightfully clever. I do say, clever indeed," he marveled. "I see why you keep her in your employ."

"Yes, that's it, she works for me. Comes in handy in . . . uh."

"Oh, I work for you now, is it?" she asked. I'd pay for that.

"Well, it's a pleasure to make your acquaintance. But as I said, there's some excitement brewing this way, perhaps the two of you would like to join me?"

"Well, Dodger was going—"

"I'd be delighted." Once again, Dodger offered her hand, this time, in escort, which Pip dutifully took. A pang hit my heart at seeing them cozy like that.

We hurried over to the Megalosaurus, the three of us wound through a growing cluster of restless onlookers. On the way, Pip explained that Pocket had taken his leave earlier for an important meeting in London Central and that Bucket was doing his best to keep the crowd calm here.

A low, guttural growl reverberated from the statue. No, not from it. From a point behind it, perhaps. Or from beyond the ridge. With low sounds, the source was hard to discern. It was deep and dangerous, like a crocodile at water's edge and we were standing on the shore.

The noise grew and the crowd grew anxious with it. A sudden eagerness of shoving bodies gave way to excited ooohs and ahhhs that drowned out Inspector Bucket's admonishing cries for calm.

"No phonograph player is that good, is it?" Dodger asked.

The ground shook. The low roar engulfed us, rattling our insides.

"I don't think that's part of the exhibit." Even trembling, Pip's posture rivaled a broomstick. A silent hush swept through the crowd, like a chill autumn wind.

Through the trees, over the ridge, a toothy maw appeared first, followed by the top half of a lizard-like creature covered in . . . *feathers?* One clawed foot crashed down, then another, shattering the concrete statue. Chunks of concrete and brick flew out into the crowd. Steel bars bent. Tiles exploded into fine powder.

There was a familiarity to the creature, the narrow snout, the curved razor teeth, the eyes . . . it was Pip that confirmed my suspicions.

"I told you it stood on two feet!"

I gulped. Somehow, there was an angry Megalosaurus in front of us. I eyed the others, knowing it would be up to the three of us to figure out where it had come from and to stop its rampage before anyone was killed.

Chapter 5
Running and Screaming

The Megalosaurus had burst through the bushes with a gut-punching growl. It didn't roar like a lion, but rather it released a staccato pulse-like noise that punched through my chest like no animal I'd ever heard.

"What the hell is that?" Dodger yelled out the question over the reverberations of the beast.

"I think that's a dinosaur, a Megalosaurus," I said. It looked part bird, part lizard, and all monster. Where its statue had sat squat-like on all fours, this beast balanced its body between two enormous legs, with a tail flowing freely on one end and a fierce, sharp-tooth filled jaw on the other.

The head was a reddish crocodilian patch of scales and scars, and most of its body was quilled in some sort of weird porcupine-looking spines which blended into black and deep garnet-red, like an exotic never-before-seen tropical parrot. The creature's feet and gangly little arms and tip of its tail were scaled. Its eyes were narrow and beady, and pointed our way, as if sizing us up for snacks.

The crowd pressed into each other in their attempt to flee. Instead of escape, there was a wall of immobile bodies behind us. The danger came on two fronts: a panicked mass of people who threatened to crush and trample each other, and the monster that threatened to make meals of us all. The curved, sickle-like teeth kept my attention, though it scarcely needed them with us. Its maw looked big enough to swallow any one of us whole.

Dodger stuttered out, "That's supposed to be here, right? Please tell me that this is part of the exhibition. Maybe it got out of its cage?"

Chances are, as I knew all too well, this creature's arrival likely involved time-travel. I had work to do, since that was my department. I had to find out how to stop this thing, how to send it back, and who brought it here in the first place. Honestly, the last chore seemed much easier than the first two by comparison.

So far, the creature simply stood there, as if perplexed. So far, so good. Let it puzzle us out instead of having us for tea.

"It can't have escaped." Pip pulled us all back into the crowd as much as they would give, his arms stretching across us like a barrier. There had to be a hundred of us or so, men, women and children, and their panic was going to get someone hurt – or worse. Pip continued, as if out for a Sunday stroll, not a care in the world and very fascinated by the thing that might kill him. "Dinosaurs are extinct. Did you know the word means 'terrible lizard'?"

"That looks nothing like a lizard," Dodger said. I couldn't have agreed more. "Looks more like fifteen-foot-tall bird to me. With the head of a crocodile."

"Maybe they're terrible at being lizards?" I offered.

The Megalosaurus belched out another rhythmic rumble. Its throat, which I now noticed as bright red, undulated with each successive wave. The ground shook as it took another step closer to us, fully demolishing the Megalosaurus statue underfoot.

I gulped.

Finally, the crowd got it together. The solid wall started to crumble as people peeled off, screaming, in every direction. The three of us, plus a flustered Chief Inspector, were pushed and shoved, but we held our ground as I tried to come up with a plan.

"We need to get these people to safety." I directed. This was my job, I assumed. Of course, I should have remembered whose company I was in.

"No, they'll sort themselves out." Pip pointed with his cane to the dinosaur. His movement with his cane reminded me that I held a few surprises in mine, should the need arise. "We need to get this creature to safety and out of the way of anyone that might hurt it. That's our aim, Oliver."

"You're seriously siding with that thing?" Dodger raised a brow. She sounded incredulous, and a little angry too. "Oliver, the foundlings: Abbey, Edward, Byron. They're inside. Your first order is to get them to safety."

That Dodger's first instinct had changed to the children's welfare, rather than her own, surprised me. But there wasn't time to consider that now. There was a dinosaur on a rampage, and this was not going to end well.

Bucket chose that moment to rush over. He gave Dodger the once over before making the decision to prioritize. There was, after all, bigger game afoot. "I must take my leave to rally the uniforms. When I do, we'll be at your disposal, Mr. Twist."

Odd. And quite uncomfortable, to be honest.

"Also," he continued, "If your friend is still here when I return with reinforcements, I'm taking her in. The book the yard has on her would rival Scrooge's ledgers."

Dodger tipped her hat. Always the classy one. As the Inspector made his own path through the crowd, Dodger confronted me, likely in a bid to make a hasty exit before Bucket made good on his promise. "Don't go with Pip. The foundlings are your family."

"They're in good hands with you," I said. They were, but what was I saying? The choice between Dodger and Pip, and the responsibility that Bucket had dished, weighed heavily on me. But I had to decide now. More often than not, my delays and second-guessing had gotten people hurt. It was my biggest weakness.

Pip pulled my arm, leading me out of the crowd, but Dodger threaded alongside, urging me to reconsider. As the throng of well-dressed men and women threatened to separate us, she called out, "Oliver!"

I shook my head. "Get the children to—"

Gunpowder cracked, punctuating the roar of the creature and the screams of the crowd with a strange moment of silence. Acrid grey smoke hung in the air directing me to the source of the shot. The redcoat, likely on loan from the nearby Wellington barracks, stood firm. But that courage was going to get him killed.

Either the shot missed the dinosaur, or it shrugged off the wound. Its steely eyes bore into the soldier like bayonets. British soldiers wore red to hide their injuries from their enemies, but no amount of red cloth could hide a wound from this beast. I pulled away from Pip, pressing forward toward the soldier before his breeches turned brown.

I didn't make it in time.

Like a hawk swooping down on a field mouse, the soldier was gone before I could blink. The dinosaur stepped forward, lunging at the soldier with a wide-open mouth, it picked him up and swallowed him whole, all in one smooth, bird-like motion. All I could see of the man were limp legs and all I could hear was his muffled scream.

"Still think Abbey and the others are safe?" Dodger caught up to me, clasping her hands on my shoulders, her face white as a ghost. "After that?" I had Pip on one side and Dodger on the other and, in the middle, a choice to make.

But first, I had to save the soldier's life. My indecisions, uncertainty, my second-guessing myself, was counterbalanced by my timepiece. I might still be able to help, even though the soldier was dead – such was the power at my disposal.

However, the thing about time-travel is that there are constants, set events in time that cannot be altered. There were also arbitrary rules that had to be followed and that were always changing. And finally, prices to be paid; for nothing, especially bending the rules of time, came without consequences.

I hated it, for I never knew exactly what I could fix and what I couldn't or how far back I could travel. Every trip was different. I was only an instrument, to be used at the whim of the Fates, a ship with no oar or rudder, bound to the currents.

I had to try. My hands shook as I fumbled to fish out the timepiece.

"We've got to go now," Pip pleaded. "I know what we need. But I need your help to get it. Will you come?"

I didn't answer. Pip and Dodger wouldn't remember this conversation anyway. Because it would never happen. Time-travel worked that way, though it was hard for me to remember what others didn't, since I remembered everything.

Before the dinosaur could pick out dessert, I finally pulled my pocket watch free from my waistcoat. I hadn't used it since Scrooge's salvation, for I'd been warned against using it again too soon. The veil between the spirit realm and ours had been breached last Christmas and, ironically, the Fates and Spirits that guided my travels needed *time* to sort it out. Here goes everything.

Oliver. It's me, Ne—

A faint, almost distant voice, barely recognizable, nicked the back of my brain. Or did it come from the watch? Before the voice could speak again, the dinosaur bellowed and hurtled towards me.

I no longer needed to twist the pinion of the watch. Simply holding it and focusing in on what I needed enabled me to tap into the streams of the Spirits that controlled it. With growing copper swirls of lights and flashes swirling around the watch and encircling me, I aimed to speed back into the past, intent on saving the soldier.

I ducked as the dinosaur's knife-like teeth shut around me—

"Oliver, time to use your timepiece," I heard Pip say distantly as I faded from view and out of harm's way. "Oh, I wanted to see this! Good sport, ol' chap!"

So, not only did he (and most of London) know about my vigilantism, he also knew about my watch. How did he know about that? There was no time to consider it as I popped back into the past.

***

Crack!

Copper colors faded as the circle slowly diminished. I caught the whiff of powder and the echoes of the musket blast. Bollocks. That didn't give me much time. Already, the dinosaur was sizing up his meal, narrowing his eyes on the tasty prize. The crowd pressed around me, with Pip on one side and Dodger on the other, like two shoulder angels.

I spied a four-way lamppost, wrought-iron with unlit gaslights jutting out along each junction of the pathway, affixed to a small granite block. It was my only chance to counter the crowd because I'd never reach him in time even if I plowed through them.

Ungracefully, I rushed over and leapt onto the lamppost, hanging on with one hand and one foot on the stone. I looked like a monkey hanging from a metal tree waving around a cane. That cane, however, held a surprise. It had gotten me out of many tight corners such as this before.

The dinosaur lunged at the soldier as I pressed a hidden button on my cane. It launched an air-powered ball of brass (connected on a line of strong wire filament) at the soldier. The bulb shot out and past his chest and wrapped around him as teeth-filled jaws barreled down. I pulled with all my strength, jumping off the block and wrapping my end of the cord around the lamppost for better leverage.

The cord went taut and caught the soldier, yanking him out of the way as the Megalosaurus ate the space where he'd stood. The dinosaur's head jerked upwards, its eyes searching, but it seemed confused enough for now to leave us alone. The soldier returned a shaky nod, the cord retracting from around him and returning to my cane.

I had saved the soldier – for now. But that didn't mean that my actions were without consequence – I'd lost too many people I loved, so I knew better. One of those people that I had deeply cared about, Mr. Brownlow, once told me that I couldn't save everyone. It turns out, he'd been right.

"Jolly good show, that one," Pip called from below. I had to remind myself that he knew more than he let on. "Shall we get this strange creature to safety?"

Right. For a bird, it bellowed instead of chirped. The dinosaur made as much sense as a platypus. But what was sensical about any of this? Where in the blazes had it come from anyway?

"Everybody, into the building," I called. After my so-called heroics, people listened, urged on and directed by the soldier as the dinosaur looked on with uncertainty.

"People are panicking, and you're sending them into a building made of glass?" Dodger admonished. Put that way, Dodger had a point. But some shelter was better than nothing, surely? There were a few brick outbuildings dotting the landscape, but those were only large enough to hold one or two people at best. The Palace was reinforced with iron. It had to hold while we shepherded the creature away.

"It'll have to do." I hoped.

"The Palace is crowded enough," Dodger argued, "It doesn't have enough exits. If the glass breaks, especially the roof, everyone's at risk. More importantly, the foundlings are in there."

"Oliver's the hero, he makes the rules, don't you?" Pip said in a way that made it sound like he was pulling the strings. Maybe he was, but I didn't like that.

"Listen here, you pipsqueak—" Dodger waved a fist.

"Get the children away from here. Pip and I will draw off the dinosaur."

Dodger returned a hard stare that would rival the look Medusa gave the Kraken. "You're making a mistake."

"Do what you do best, dodge trouble." I shook my head and left her there, joining Pip. It hurt to refuse Dodger's call. But I wanted to trust him, which meant that what I needed to do was to keep my eyes peeled.

The dinosaur charged, as the crowds finally fled, further separating us. Dodger corralled the others inside while I raced with Pip toward his hansom cab. I kept looking back. "Where are we going? What if the dinosaur eats someone again? I won't be there."

"Save the dinosaur, save the people, you need to see the larger picture." Pip plowed ahead with me in tow. "Besides, we can't save everybody—"

"Wait, what did you say?" I shuddered inwardly. Pip's words sent alarm bells ringing warning me of a man far more dangerous than a dinosaur.

Chapter 6
The Stinger

Racing away with Pip from the destructive dinosaur and ditching Dodger pulled at every bit of common sense I had, which admittedly, wasn't much. My very soul screamed to go back, but I shook away the feeling. I trusted that the foundlings would be safe with Dodger. And Pip, well, he saw more clearly than I did.

I must embrace a larger view, as it were, if I were to step up in London's society and ally myself with Pip and his peers. But—

We can't save them all. His words rolled around in my head, like dice coming up snake eyes. I sat uneasily in the hansom across from him, wondering how much he knew about me, how he had known about my watch, and curious how genuine his offer of partnership had been, all the while keeping track of the passing seconds on my timepiece.

It was too late to turn back now as the hansom hurried quickly to Pip's destination. But the streets were closing in with panicked pedestrians who had heard the news of a strange beast in Hyde Park. Still, our driver – a surly man with coffee breath – deftly dodged them all in a manner Dodger would envy.

I looked out at leaping pedestrians as we charged further away from the dinosaur and the foundlings. I was pale and sweaty. *What had I done?*

"You said you could help, why are we running away?" I held tightly to the wooden lip of my seat as scenes of chaos swept past my window. Pip's hansom careened through the crowded street of would-be gawkers and frightened onlookers who *had* seen the beast. You could tell by how the fear had taken root in their eyes. The ones who knew better fled, while others headed toward the greens. And the ones who got in our way leapt aside at the last moment. A large man in a pin-striped coat and cracked goggles jeered at me as our wheels narrowly missed him.

"Never mind them, they're safe. My driver is practiced and precise, even if he is a bit like curdled milk. We're on important matters. Matters that necessitate a bit of recklessness. For that, I'm glad to have you here."

What did that mean? I wasn't reck—

Oh.

"Bucket wastes time calling The Yard, they'll have no more luck against that creature than that soldier you saved. Meanwhile, we'll be resourceful, even if it seems counterintuitive at first." Pip remained calm and reflective, like freshly polished silver, while I wrapped my head around his words.

"Counter—?" I didn't know what that meant. The more I was around Pip, the more I realized I needed the aid of a dictionary and a thesaurus. Without them, I was at loss for words.

"You'll see."

The carriage sped through traffic, winding south from Hyde Park and the Crystal Palace, to central London, past Buckingham Palace and across the Thames to Walworth – I gathered our direction and destination from landmarks and sharp turns we made. As to what purpose, I still couldn't fathom. "Do we have time for this?"

Our cab veered around another corner. I think two wheels lifted off the ground as if the whole hansom threatened to take flight. By now, my knuckles were white around my cane and my light tea now resided in the upper tenement of my throat.

My host remained quiet, unbothered. His reflective look went unbroken for some time until he breached the silence with, "Ahh, we're here."

The cab slammed to a sudden stop, as if the horses had hit a wall. I lurched out of my seat, nearly ending in Pip's lap. Pip, for his part, remained statuesque. How did he do that?

We arrived at a house situated on a lonely corner in the outskirts of Walworth. But it was no mere home, it was *large* for lack of a better word. Not palatial, not ostentatious (I can use big words too, Pip) but by no means modest. The owner had constructed for himself a castle out of a *cottage?* Complete with moat, drawbridge, and some sort of cannon-like contraption sitting atop a balcony, as if protecting the place.

"Stinger, he calls it. Part cannon, part gatling. Multiple barrels for multiple threats." Pip went right from the carriage up the walk across the downed drawbridge. "It's rather loud and obnoxious, so it'll suit our purposes fine. In fact, when it fires, it's the loudest noise in all London. And Wemmick loves to fire it. It's the only thing my near-deaf friend can hear."

The contraption was placed on a parapet overlooking the pathway to the door, which meant it served as a hefty deterrent for door-to-door salesmen, preachy religious types, and un-invited relatives. I at once saw the appeal of the weapon and its placement.

Pip promptly opened a normal-looking green front door and walked right inside. I furrowed my brow and took a second look around. It didn't make sense – the lowered bridge over the moat, the unlocked door – so much for an impregnable fortress.

"Are you joining me?" Pip popped his head back out the door. I followed him inside. "I've dined here on occasion, enough to learn Wemmick's peculiarities. He only barricades himself from the world while he's home. Otherwise, it's quite open, as you can see. But there's his problem, Oliver, you can't shut out the world. Just like time, it goes on whether you want it to or not no matter where you are or how you fortify from it. Foul deeds can find you anywhere, at any time."

Inside, it was simply a home, with a cozy kitchen, comfortable sitting arrangements, dozens of bottles of wine and twice that many books. What was missing was any trace of his profession or occupation. Clearly, work was work and home was home and the two were strictly seperate. The castle idea started to make sense.

"So, we're here to steal his gatling gun?" We'd made our way to the cannon's emplacement and Pip went to work removing the chocks.

"Borrow, Oliver." I aided Pip in wheeling it away. "Surely, you've done the same when in pursuit of the greater good. Right and wrong become muddy on occasion."

Like leaving Dodger and the foundlings for a mysterious fellow I'd only just met? Maybe I shouldn't mention that. So, I said, "I've done my share of thieving."

Regardless, morality was a slippery slope. So, we needed a cannon today. What if we needed something more dangerous tomorrow? Lines in the sand can easily be washed away by a troubled tide. No, my problem was not the thieving or our wild ride. My problem was why we needed the gun in the first place. "We're going to kill the creature?"

I studied the weapon. It was a multi-barreled cannon with a rotator crank that allowed it to fire rapidly. From the length of the barrel, the train of ammunition trailing down and snaking to the ground, the weapon looked deadly.

"Of course, not." Pip looked as upset with me as if I'd kicked his puppy. We continued to roll the cannon down a specially constructed ramp, and away from the house with my awkward assistance. "The dinosaur's reverberations reminded me of the echoes this cannon makes when fired. I'm curious if firing it will frighten our friend off or lure it in. Either way, we can use Stinger here to our advantage."

It was a good plan, proof that Pip might be the man he promised. Of course, I was in favor of mounting the dinosaur in a museum if it came down to either it or my foundlings. But Pip was the enlightened one, so we'd do it his way. Once the dinosaur was contained, we could start on the larger questions, like: what was it doing here in the first place?

I patted my pocket watch. Usually, when London was under siege, my timepiece tended to be the culprit. The last time, it had been all my fault. But I didn't think that was the case in this instance.

We hitched the cannon to the back of the hansom. The thing was heavy, but there was no time to catch my breath. Pip didn't seem bothered. Then again, I recalled someone saying he'd been a blacksmith. I wondered why our driver didn't offer to help but when I shot him a questioning eye, he returned a glare that could wilt a flower. He had his lane and stuck to it, unless of course, he was driving.

As I hurried back into the carriage after Pip, questions popped in my mind. Where had our prehistoric friend come from? Was he alone or had he brought his mates? Were there other surprises for me? To the last question, I had a hunch that it was more a matter of *when*.

"Are you sure this weapon was worth the time it took?" I asked now that our deed was done. The carriage cracked forward and the horses hung a sharp turn to take us back. All that was left was to return to where we'd left, give our dinosaur a welcoming greeting, and see where things evolved from there. Easy.

"You'll have to trust me, Oliver, and take decisive action." Pip took his seat in the carriage returning to the serenity that he held with ease. "No, I retract that. You must trust yourself."

Ouch. I had hesitated in joining Pip. And I'd been second guessing my choices this entire time. *Act decisively.* He wasn't wrong. Somehow Pip had gotten into my head and that was a problem. I didn't like people poking around there. How he knew me so well remained a mystery. It might have to do with our shared backgrounds, but I thought it was more. I think he knew more than he let on, if that was even possible, Mr. Jack-of-All-Trades.

I had wanted to be like Pip, to lift myself up to the upper echelons of society, to shed my shameful street skin. But now, as we crossed the Thames and headed toward Hyde Park to track and contain the creature, I held the uneasy feeling that I was looking at this all the wrong way.

As we flew back to Hyde Park with Stinger in tow, I mulled over my thoughts. "You have to trust me," Pip had said. He hadn't done anything to betray that trust, but had he done anything to earn it? Typically, if someone has to tell you to trust them, you shouldn't.

Perhaps my instincts had been correct all along. Maybe I should have trusted myself and not pursued Pip's plan. My gut could get confused, but my heart, I realized, had been screaming at me to stay with Dodger.

One thing was certain, as our carriage bounced across the roads leading back to chaos, I was stepping into yet another situation where London and my friends were in trouble. My eyes caught Pip's, who remained as stalwart as ever, as I questioned inwardly whether I could trust him. Or if I could trust myself to save Dodger and the foundlings.

If they hadn't been eaten already.

Chapter 7
Abbey

Abbey didn't like the Crystal Palace. It was big, too big for a girl her small size. There were too many people pushing her around. She was squeezed and crowded, and she had a difficult time keeping up with the boys who kept racing ahead. And it was hot beneath the glass.

She didn't like wearing the red wool jacket she was supposed to wear over her pink and white checkered dress. So, she took it off and tied the sleeves around her waist. The grown-ups admonished her, but she didn't care. It was a girly outfit that she didn't like anyway. Miss Dodger had 'acquired' it for the occasion of today's visit and told her she only had to wear it while they were there, as she hadn't found anything else that would fit her. That was too long of a time, as far as she was concerned.

On top of everything else, her tummy growled. She hadn't eaten since they'd scarfed down stale bread and chalky cheese this morning. The greasy scent of fried chips from a food vendor across the cramped convention center called to her.

From above, the Palace was airy with a second, and in some places, a third level overlooking them. She watched as the gaggle of onlookers pointed and giggled with excited glee at the exhibits, most of which were boring. But Edward and Byron hadn't thought so, and so they'd dragged her along while Miss Dodger had stepped outside to talk with Mr. Twist.

Her attention was drawn to the far side of the room. There, several skeletons stood out like some sort of fictional monsters from fairy tales that had been read to her. When she looked back, the boys were gone.

Edward, the oldest, wore clothes like Mr. Twist: waistcoat, tie, and silver-grey frockcoat. Byron still wore the same black pants, shined shoes and the now-faded jacket he'd worn every day since his twin's funeral this last Christmas. Ever since the accident, Abbey had stuck to him like glue, she didn't want him to be alone.

They had gotten separated here, though. It was almost impossible not to. So, she searched ahead for outfits matching those descriptions. Byron's faded jacket was how she found the boys, bunched around the table of a thin mustachioed man with a flat straw hat. On display was a rack of dark-blue scarves and a glass case that housed four different canes.

But the canes were not ordinary ones. Neither were the scarves. She knew who else wore a scarf like that, but it was a secret that she promised not to tell. Mr. Twist would be very cross. Just like the scarves, the canes also looked like the ones he used.

Sure enough, the man showcased a cane from the table he had at the ready. Once he had a large enough crowd, he pressed a release on the weapon and a heavy brass ball, connected to a wire thread, popped out high into the air. It slowed and descended before reaching the glass ceiling. He sidestepped it as the brass ball plummeted beside him, cracking into the wooden flooring.

"Get your gas propelled cane, just like the one The Orphan uses, so that you can protect your loved ones, too," the man hawked. "Perfected by great British minds and introduced to you at this very Exhibition. We're taking orders now."

Edward shook his head angrily. "He can't do that, can he?"

Abbey had gotten used to seeing other children wearing blue scarves and jumping off barrels, but she didn't like the idea of grown-ups having those canes. "There has to be a rule against it, right?"

"I think it's splendid," Byron said.

"Nobody was asking you." Edward balled his hand into a fist.

Abbey scrunched between them. "Don't fight," she said. "I'm hungry."

"Of course you are." Edward took in a sniff of air and relaxed his hand. "There's food over there, but we'll have to wait for Miss Dodger to return. I don't have any coin."

Abbey's tummy growled in response. But it was a much louder growl than she had realized. In fact, it hadn't come from her stomach at all even though she had felt it in there.

"Did you feel that?" Byron asked.

"Feel it?" Edward said, "I heard it." He looked around, "Where'd that come from?"

So, it hadn't come from her, Abbey realized. They heard it again, a low, powerful, *grgrgrgr* that tickled her tummy, but she wasn't laughing. Instead, her head went light and dizzy and prickles went down her arms. "Edward, what is that?"

The boys turned in time to see a large lizard crashing through the glass wall less than ten feet away from them. Shards flew out and bits of broken, sharp glass cut Byron's face and sliced through his jacket. Edward shoved him back as he sheltered Abbey from the flying debris.

People screamed and ran. They pushed past the three of them, threatening to topple them to the ground. She risked a glance as the monster came closer. She could see now that it was covered in red and black feathers. She thought it strange, but there were so many things here in the Palace that were new and different that for a moment, she almost felt fascinated. But as the beast growled again, that feeling fled.

"Under here, quick." Edward pulled the red tablecloth from the man's booth high enough for them to slink underneath. The man himself was gone, and with all the people rushing away it would have been impossible for them to make their escape. She would have been trampled and crushed underfoot had they tried. Grown-ups didn't care for people her size.

Edward was right, Abbey realized. Hiding was their only option. She dove under the table as Byron joined her, wiping away the trail of blood running across his cheek. Edward took the front spot, laying with both hands pressed against the floor, his eyes peeking out from the small gap between the edge of the tablecloth and the floor.

For the longest time, all Abbey could hear was the yelling of adults and the cries of children like herself and the slapping of shoe-leather on the floor as people raced past the table. She couldn't see anything, but that was mostly because she didn't want to, her eyes were closed, and her head was tucked between both arms. On the occasions where she did peek, she saw only Byron and hurried shadows.

The monster growled again, a reverberation that beat across an emptying room. With each step it took, it seemed to her as if every pane of glass shook. Everyone else must have fled by now, she imagined that it was just the scary monster and the three of them.

Maybe it was. The monster was coming closer. Could it smell them? Were they making too much noise? She took a risk and saw that part of their hiding place was exposed, the tablecloth hadn't settled down at the far end of the table. The large lizard looked right at them . . .

And lowered its large head to the floor.

Abbey screamed. It was a blood-curdling, high-pitched scream that she hadn't thought herself capable of making. She hadn't meant to either, it had screeched out of her lungs and shot out of her mouth.

"Quiet," Edward snapped. But it was too late, the creature knew where they were. "Out the back, now."

Byron began pushing Abbey out, but she was frozen in place. The creature's head pushed underneath the table. Edward scooted down, away from its mouth, but the monster tracked him. Edward hit it on the snout to no effect.

Its jaw snapped open, grabbing Edward by his right arm. He yelped in surprise as his sleeve got snagged onto a tooth. The monster began to pull Edward out from underneath the table. Byron and Abbey both grabbed onto his other arm, pulling him back, but the creature's grip was too strong for them.

In the shuffle, the table toppled over. The edge hit Abbey in the head. She went woozy as she climbed out from underneath. The display case of canes came crashing down. She ducked out of the way, her head spinning, while the case of canes crashed onto the ground. The glass case shattered. The canes rolled wildly with one of them stopping near Abbey's feet, but just beyond her reach.

The tablecloth wrapped around the creature's snout. Scarves flew out like billowing banners of blue. Still, the monster did not let go of Edward as he and Byron tried to beat it back.

It eyed Abbey, its red pupil bore into her like the darkest creatures of her dreams. If Edward died, she wouldn't sleep at all, maybe never. There wouldn't be any dreams. She had to save him. But first, she had to stop her hands from trembling.

Edward was crying, his arm twisting as he tried to writhe away. There was a reptilian glint in this monster's eye that gave Abbey cold chills. She had to shake it off, be big and brave, she told herself. She hadn't much time.

"Abbey," Byron pushed her away, "run, get help." She toppled over and hit the floor hard. At first, she was going to yell at him for pushing her, but she realized that she was within reach of one of the stupid man's makeshift canes. She grabbed it, quickly rose, and aimed.

She pressed the button, and the brass ball, like Mr. Twist's weapon, shot out at the animal's eye. It hit dead center. "Take that, you big meanie!"

It let go of Edward, dropping him a foot onto the floor. He collapsed in a ball as the monster jerked its huge head away. It took a few steps in retreat and rumbled loudly as if in pain. She hadn't meant to hurt it, but it was hurting her friend. Byron pulled Edward up, and the three raced away.

"This way," Abbey yelled. She directed them toward a series of rooms with wooden doors against the far edge of the building. Dodger had taken her there earlier when she had to pee. It was explained to her that these were new flushing toilets both on exhibition and for use. That didn't matter to her now, she just sought shelter.

They plowed through the door and raced into the smelly loo, but it was preferable to the stink of rotten flesh she had caught from the monster. Byron slammed the door closed behind them. Edward collapsed to the ground, clutching his arm. The sleeve had been torn away and his skin was red and swollen, but the arm was still there.

The room was barely big enough for the three of them. There was an oval bucket-like bowl behind them with a tubular water tank above and a pedal on the floor for flushing. There wasn't much else except for a glass window high above them.

If the beast came for them, they would be trapped.

There was stillness for the longest time. Tears ran from Abbey's eyes. She was afraid for Edward, who was pale and sweaty. Byron was bleeding from his hands and face. She couldn't hear the monster anymore, but she imagined it right outside the door.

"What do we do if it comes back for us?" she asked.

The boys did not answer. Their silence served to scare her even more. That was, until the door handle rattled. Abbey jumped back, bumping into the toilet bucket. It was over, the monster had them, they were all going to be eaten like Edward had almost been—

The door flew open, but shadows obscured the figure.

"I caught sight of you running toward the Monkey Closets," the voice said.

"Miss Dodger?" she asked, as if it couldn't possibly be true.

It was. She scooped Abbey up into her arms and with a gentle whispering, she said, "You're safe now."

Chapter 8
A Visitor from the Future

The carriage came to an abrupt stop not too far from where we'd set off. At first, I thought our over-coffee'd driver had hit something but soon I realized the reason for stopping so suddenly. There was an approaching rumbling, like that of a train, coming from . . . the sky?

A terrible noise broke from the clouds, but it wasn't thunder. Pressing both hands tightly against my ears, Pip and I flew out of the carriage to investigate. The horses kicked and brayed but were unable to close their ears with their hooves. Poor creatures.

Pip pointed upward at an angular, metallic craft roaring past. Made from steel, perhaps? Shaped almost like an arrow, but with long wings at the midpoint and a fin at the back. Windows dotted the sides, and red paint outlined the otherwise white object. Whatever it was didn't look like it ran on any sort of steam-power that I knew.

It flew low, as large round wheels descended from the body of the craft. I could make out the words 'British Airways' written on its side. So, it was an air-transport of some sort, not dissimilar from the steam-powered airships that floated dreamily across the sky. Those at least, were quiet. How could anyone travel in such a slender, noisy, metal tube like that?

"I'd wondered if the dinosaur was the only thing displaced in time," I said to Pip, as the aero-craft passed and we could talk again. I'd heard of inventors from the time of Da Vinci toying with the idea of flight. This was much more advanced, so I assumed it came from the future. This meant that our dinosaur was not a one-off.

There was a problem with time itself. So, it would be up to me to figure this out and fix it. Fancy that.

"I'll take another ten monsters on the ground rather than whatever that was," Pip yelled, his hearing obviously still not right. He was also visibly shaking. It only took futuristic air travel to shake him.

The flying craft descended out of sight, possibly landing in some empty farmer's field in Heathrow. The roar was gone. The horses calmed and the usual sounds of people panicking resumed.

"So, this problem is bigger than we thought," I said, for the benefit of Pip.

"Larger is the word you're looking for," Pip clapped me on the shoulder. "And agreed, ol' chap. Luckily, we've got you."

No pressure. I worried that I was once again outmatched. Time, as I had learned from experience, was never on my side.

***

Speaking of time not being on my side, retrieving Stinger had eaten twenty minutes off the clock. But we were back in the park . . . again. Hyde Park was, to no surprise, much emptier than when we'd left it. How much damage had the Megalosaurus caused in our absence and where was it right now? I eyed the gatling gun warily. We may now have the means to lure the dinosaur, but I still wasn't convinced that it was our best course of action. But first, we had to find it.

"Who would win in a fight, dinosaurs or machines?"

"What?" I asked. Pip had a way of breaking me from my thoughts, but this was strange, even for him.

"There are steam-powered machines showcased at the exhibition. We were supposed to see them on our tour," Pip checked his own timepiece and clicked it shut. "Right about now. We missed out. So, I'm curious, what do you think would win: the past or future?"

"Oh." I gave Pip a puzzled look as we unhooked the gatling gun and rolled it over the greens toward the last known location of the Megalosaurus. There was wreckage ahead. "I don't know."

"Robots, for my money," Pip gestured at the gatling gun we'd brought, still heavy as ever and not getting any lighter lugging it around. "Technology always triumphs."

I wasn't sure about that. The past had a way of creeping up on you, like a swift and sudden storm.

We returned to the Crystal Palace. The center arboretum with its mighty elm and the wing where I'd placed flowers remained intact. But the wing we toured was in ruins. If Dodger and the foundlings had been here . . .

Dust from the wreckage swirled around us, clouding my eyes and making them water and itch. I had to squint to see. And what I could see didn't instill confidence that I'd made the right choice to go with Pip. We wheeled the weapon to a stop and took stock.

What had once been palatial was now shards of glass and twisted metal, like the shattering of millions of jars. But I was more concerned for anyone who may have been caught inside. I didn't see anyone, or any remains, yet. I breathed out heavily, thanking Dodger and her bag of tricks for keeping everyone alive and hopefully, uninjured.

There was a trickle of blood that trailed into the wreckage, but that might have been from the dinosaur itself and not from its victims. I remembered its wound from the soldier, though I had to think back to recall if our beasty had been shot in the new timeline I had created, and I thought that he had. Maybe.

"Dinosaurs or robots?" I asked. "You see what this dinosaur has done, don't you?"

Pip and I rounded the corner of the shattered glass wall. Iron catwalks hung suspended loosely above us like skeletal remains while broken glass was piled like molted skin. Having grown up without shoes, I was glad for them now as sharp shards crunched underfoot.

But our attention was drawn to a small brick structure nearby, off the path. It was one of the many outbuildings that housed the infrastructure for the ornate facility, most probably for plumbing, or steam-power. No larger or taller than a carriage, it would have been too full of pipes for anyone to have used as shelter, except perhaps for someone small or slender, like a child. *Like a foundling.* The thought had me worried as we hurried to it.

The structure leaned against itself, threatening to topple over at any second, as if the dinosaur had slammed into it, knocking it off its foundation and leaving it ready for collapse.

"But robots would have weapons, lasers, even," Pip said. I knew at once he was attempting to distract me from whatever horrors we might find inside.

"Lasers?" I questioned, thankful and annoyed by him at the same time. "What in the Dickens is a laser?"

"Hello?" A wavering, soft voice crept out of the makeshift brick cave, cutting off Pip before he could answer my question. The door was wedged shut. Loose bricks fell before our eyes. The building was collapsing. I'd seen the results of a tunnel cave-in once and I still carried the scars in my heart to this day.

"We've got to get her out of there." Pip charged in, nary a thought to his own danger. Perhaps there was a glint of a hero in him, after all. But it was suicide, not rescue. It was a cheap wooden door, not reinforced in any way. It gave way under Pip's charge, and so did the rest of the building.

"Pip, no—"

It was too late. My warning went unheeded as the walls, made from yellowish London stock brick, collapsed inward, entombing both Pip and the woman with him. The building may not have looked like much, but the force and weight of the wall, and steel pipes inside, planted a grotesque image in my head.

They hadn't even screamed. But they had been crushed. I hoped they hadn't suffered. I remembered Farley, the boy who had succumbed slowly after the tunnel cave-in. Shaky hands, heart racing, I couldn't hold my timepiece still enough to erase what had happened here soon enough.

Bits of brick dust stung my eyes and burned my throat. I dropped to the ground, dropping my timepiece in the process. From my belly, I clawed blindly, searching the rubble for my watch. I grasped a warm and round object. Flipping it open, I felt the bask of energy whisking me away to the safety of the past.

***

"Oliver," a familiar voice came again as I was being sent back, "Lasers are a tool of the future—"

The future? Why would Pip know of the future? And why would that voice, I knew that voice, take the time to warn me about that? None of that was important to me right now. Thoughts turned to action as my Pip-less future became the past.

***

My eyes were free of brick dust but full of haze from the destruction of the Crystal Palace. Pip was back at my side, facing the same structure as before.

"We've got to get inside." Pip pressed on but I held him back. He eyed me suspiciously, his shoulders stiffened, poising to pull away. After his eyes lit up, he softened and asked, "Did I die? Did you use your watch?"

I nodded.

In truth, that hadn't been the first time. Nor the second. We'd done this before many times, but I wanted to skip ahead.

Pip would rip open the door, charge in, and the building would collapse. I'd turn back time and he'd do it again.

Finally, I'd caught his coattails and kept him from being reckless. Pip might have been intelligent, but he was also brash, and, in this case, his brain lost out to his brawn.

It must have been the woman's voice pleading for help, but his chivalrous attempts at rescuing the damsel kept getting them both mangled. I didn't tell him any of that, and I don't wish to repeat the details here. All I said to Pip was, "We need a better plan."

"I see," Pip coughed. "Thanks for that, but if we don't do something soon, our fair lady inside won't survive."

The building's walls gave way. They didn't fall in slow motion like a line of dominoes. It was in an instant, the building was there one moment, and then it wasn't. In its place was a cloud of dust and bits of brick everywhere.

"Agreed," I coughed. Damn the Spirits of Past, Present and Future, they didn't give me enough time. They never gave me enough time. I needed help to change her fate. I'd been eyeing a long, twisted piece of iron from the wreckage of the Palace on the path nearby during each of our failed attempts and trips back in time. It might work . . .

I fetched the metal bar. It was both heavy and cold and hard to balance, let alone carry.

"What are you doing?"

"Something I haven't tried in a while. Let's hope it works," I answered, flipping my watch open. Copper colors bathed me once more and sped me backwards to those crucial moments. After the coppery field dissipated, I found myself standing at the entrance of the brick building once more.

"Time-travel?" Pip asked me quizzically. His eyes were raised, and he considered the bar in my hand, which from his point of view had simply materialized there. "Where'd you get that?"

"No time to explain. Get the door."

Pip tore it open as I jammed the beam into place. "Pull her out quick!"

I don't think Pip liked not having answers, but sensing my urgency, he rushed in toward the woman. She was trapped between the wall and green steel pipes the diameter of a cheese wheel. While he rescued her, I kept the bar wedged into the entrance, trying to cement it in place, but it was a losing effort, I could only buy the two a moment. If the building collapsed onto the three of us, there would be no do-overs.

The bar bent, but as the bricks crashed down, two figures emerged, covered in a reddish-yellow film of dust. Pip's finery was all but ruined. Coughing, I helped pull the two out and away from the collapsing structure.

There's never enough time. Bricks and mortar and dust buried the spot where we stood a moment before. That was a bit close.

A whisper-like voice, said, "There was time enough once the two of you worked together."

Great. My watch was talking to me. Or I was hearing voices. I rubbed the tip of my finger in each ear. I think all that did was to rub more stuff in.

Tears cleared irritated eyes and soon I could see my companions. Pip had lost his hat, a cardinal sin for a gentleman. His dusky blond hair was saturated with bricky bits and mortar. The girl was smaller than Pip, with curly dark hair, and strange clothes, including . . . trousers?

"Dinosaurs." She coughed, choking on the word while answering Pip's question. She must have heard our discussion.

Pip searched around in desperation for his silk top hat. He didn't even brush himself off. He found it, saw that it was flattened, and gave it a swift kick down the path. It didn't skid far. He told no one in particular, "I should've brought the bowler."

"Sorry about your hat, Pip. And, not to pour salt on the wound, it looks like dinosaurs have it, two to one." Not that I was invested in the argument (although making multiple trips back through time afforded me extra time to think. It was like when you're at a loss for an argument, and you think of one later whilst in the bath). I wanted to break the heavy air that seemed to have fallen between us while we were all catching our breath. "Machines might pack a punch, but eventually they'll run out of steam."

The bad joke was worth it for Pip's groan alone. Our new companion didn't laugh. Either it wasn't funny (ouch) or she was from a time that didn't use steam-power. She lacked goggles or gears on her clothing which seemed to confirm this. Instead, she had on a brown overcoat over denim trousers and a red blousy shirt. The clothes were unusual for women to wear in our time. No corsets or petticoats here. Clearly, fashion was different wherever she was from. Nell would have approved.

A wallet of some fashion had fallen on the ground. It matched the same brown material and color of her jacket. Pip picked it up. It opened to reveal a white rectangular card with a photograph of the woman. But the picture completely betrayed the woman's smile, fierce dark eyes, and wispy eyebrows. Were cameras broken in the future?

"Miss Estella Havisham, of University Hall, I presume?" Pip had read the card aloud for her name and residence. He took Stella's hand in his and kissed it. Pip was laying it on thick, even for an Englishman. I gagged a little.

"I am. But just Stella." She took the wallet and placed it somewhere inside her jacket. Nell appreciated pockets – I wish she were here to see this. They would have a lot in common. Stella continued the courtship with, "Aren't you the gentleman?"

"It is with every fiber of my being that I strive to be, madam." He bowed. "It is a pleasure to meet such a beautiful woman. I'm sorry it had to be under these unfortunate circumstances."

I wanted to gag again but the well had run empty. My mouth was still dry from all the dust about. Perhaps Pip needed a swift kick in the arse but before I acted, he rose.

"You saved me," she said. "I would have died."

He saved you? You died. Many times. The magical watch had saved you. *My* magical watch.

Stella, by all appearances, was athletic, black, with dark eyes to match. Those eyes bore solely into Pip. I might well have been on the moon rather than three feet away. "Uh, we have a dinosaur to stop." I cleared my throat. "We should be going."

"After you tell me what the hell the plan is," Stella snapped at me. Her demeanor shifted from soft to sharp in an instant. Even Pip seemed taken aback. Seeing this, she softened again. *What did I do?*

Stella sounded American. New York, maybe? I couldn't tell Yankee accents, they all came out too briskly, as if Yanks were in a rush to speak.

I answered while Pip lost himself in her gaze. "You're going to be in for quite a shock, I'm afraid, Miss Stella."

"*Stella.* No, I have the basics. I'm in the past. Time is breaking down. There's a Megalosaurus running around what looks like Victorian London and you two have some sort of plan to fix it?" Stella asked as if it wasn't a question, like she was a factory foreman expecting quotas to be met. Well, I knew now who was really in charge.

"What I want to know is if either of you two walking White Male Privileges have any idea of how to get me back home? I have exams, an upcoming production of *Hamlet* where I play Ophelia and my rent is due. You know how hard it is to find an affordable place to rent in the city?"

"You got it in one. Except for the plan part. Pip's the planner."

"Don't look at me," Pip explained. "I'm here to look pretty and rescue damsels. Twist here is the one with the gadgets and plans."

"Wait, Twist?" Stella seemed confused. "Like Oliver Twist from the book?"

"It's a long story," I said.

"Longer than 400 pages?" Stella said, "Who are you supposed to be, 'Pip'? Your book is even longer."

"I am at your service." Pip mimicked doffing his missing cap. "But there's no book about me."

"There will be after this," I assured him. It wouldn't be accurate, but writers couldn't be trusted with the truth. "Here's the plan—"

"Find the dinosaur, stop it, find whatever brought me here, and send me back," Stella said. "Where do we start?"

"I like her." Pip said.

"That was my plan." I shrugged, feeling like a third wheel in my own story. "But we're forgetting about Dodger. Did you happen to see a dark-haired lady, wears a tilted cap, with a few foundlings, er, children, with her?"

"I don't think so," Stella reflected. "I was walking out of a café and suddenly, I'm here. A lady with a strange accent was yelling at me to take cover but everything was so strange, I didn't listen. That's when I saw the Megalosaurus and flight kicked in. I raced for the building where you two found me."

"How do you know what sort of dinosaur it was?" Pip asked.

"Megalosaurus? A Jurassic era dinosaur, smaller than a Tyrannosaur, unless it was a baby Rex."

"That thing was small?" I asked.

"What's a Tyran— what did you call it?"

Pip and I stared at her.

"What? Dinosaurs are popular. There's like a billion movies about them. Plus, my roommate is a huge nerd. All she posts on Tik Tok are dinosaur facts. No dances, just her standing there in a stupid hat talking."

"What's a—" I shook my head resigning myself that I'd never understand ninety percent of whatever she said. "I don't want to know." The lady with the accent was probably Dodger. Look at her helping others, a hero in the making. My heart beamed. What was that? Was I proud of her? Maybe there were confused feelings there too. "Which way did she go?"

"I didn't see," Stella said sadly. "I'm sorry. I'm sure she's okay. I think the dinosaur went away after its fun here."

Pip had been keeping silent, which I'd found unusual even in my short time of knowing him. He was picking up the trail of blood that we had been following earlier.

"Tell me that's still from our creature," I asked him. I assumed it was, but I also didn't want to think where else that blood could have come from.

"I'm no expert," Pip stood where the dinosaur had been when it knocked into the building, "but I believe our beasty is heading north."

"Then we can follow it," Stella said. "I'm coming with you."

"Madam, that's quite out of the question," Pip said. I stayed out of the argument; I knew where this was going. Stella didn't argue either, she gave him a stony-faced look that made the case for her. Her face softened when Pip course corrected with, "I've changed my mind, it would be a pleasure to have you along. Shall we?"

"Let's go," I instructed. We'd spent too long away and every moment not tracking our quarry was more time for it to cause more harm. Pip held out his arm and Stella wrapped her hands around it. The two walked side-by-side in the direction of the gatling gun. They got along swimmingly, a real Romeo and Juliet romance blossoming before my eyes. Let's hope it didn't end in everyone's death like it did in the play.

A spear whistled past Pip's ear. All hope for a peaceful interlude vanished as another pointy death-stick sailed over my head. The tip was iron, angular, and sharp. The shaft was straight and wooden, wrapped in cloth at the handholds.

"Guys," Stella pointed to a group of a dozen warriors forming around the gatling gun as if inspecting it. *Our* gatling gun. One of them bent down to ready the weapon, as if he'd already known or had figured out how it worked. The warriors looked battle-hardened and ready to fight. Each one carried a shield made from hide, oval and as large as they were. Some carried weapons like the ones thrown at us. But the rest held wide-bladed stabbing spears. "We have a new problem."

Pip puzzled out, "Zulus?"

Chapter 9
Zulu Dawn

The gatling gun opened fire.

There was no time to contemplate our new visitors before diving behind shelter, the same outbuilding that had collapsed. But the rubbled remains were keeping us safe from the red-hot lead projectiles screaming our way. The bullets hit the bricks behind us with explosive, hammer-like blows.

I needed a plan, and I needed it now. If they kept this up and decided to encircle us, we'd be dead long before I even knew to turn back time. But who were these warriors and why were they trying to kill us?

"The Zulus?" Stella asked. "Like Shaka Zulu in *Civilization?*" None of those words made any sense to me. "It's a compu-," Stella shook her head. "You know what? Forget it. I just know that they don't like the British. And never play against them. You'll lose."

Well, that explained everything. Except who Zulus were and why they hated us – nevermind, there was plenty of reasons to loathe the British. But, you know, if it wasn't for us, everyone would be speaking French, right?

"They're hard to beat, you say? That gives me an idea," I said, finally feeling like I was contributing, "what if we get them to pursue us while we chase after our dinosaur?"

"And what would that accomplish? Oh, I see," Pip realized. His brow furrowed. "Do we want them fighting each other in the city streets?"

The gun stopped firing. They shouted at us in a language I didn't understand, someone barked out what sounded like a series of rapid commands. I could have sworn a couple of words were in English.

"No, once they see what we're up against, that we share a common problem, we find a way to recruit them. Somehow."

"That's what I meant. I don't want anyone hurt, including them or our dinosaur," Pip said. Stella smiled at that.

"I agree," I said. My plan stood a chance of working, assuming one of them spoke enough English and we could get close enough to explain everything. Unfortunately, they had Pip's gun, which meant that we were in no position to negotiate. "I'm going to turn back time, give us a better position to flee from so we're not poked full of holes."

"Turn back time?" Stella asked.

"It's a thing he does," Pip answered. "We all have our specialties. You have your brains and beauty, I stand around and look dashing."

"You're wasted in this century." Stella held up a rectangular object, as if we were supposed to know what that was. "You should write dating profiles."

"Is that how one courts where you're from, my lady?"

"Only when you talk like that." Stella smiled; her wispy eyebrows lifted above bright eyes. "But I don't woo easily. I've never once been in love."

"A challenge, then."

"Focus," I interrupted. "Dinosaur, Zulus, Dodger and the foundlings. We have work to do, Romeo." In truth, I didn't mind their banter and nascent feelings; it reminded me of what was truly important. I wanted to make sure Dodger was safe and I also missed Nell.

Both had their own way of escaping tricky situations. Dodger with her namesake evasion, Nell with her inventions. I wondered what they would do. Probably something unpredictable. Well, let's try untried and untested, shall we? What could go wrong? Where they relied on their wits and brains, I relied on my watch. "I'm changing the plan. I'm going to slip us all back in time, so we'll all remember what we're supposed to do. But it might not work."

"What's the worst that could happen?" Pip rightfully asked.

"Oh, we could all be erased from existence," I lied. I didn't really know. My pocket watch was still mostly a mystery. The usual rules allowed me, and anything connected to me – clothes, cane, watch, etc. to travel with me in time. This was fortunate, as it would do no good to turn up at Piccadilly Circle bare-arsed.

Furthermore, when I traveled back through my lifetime, I left no trace of another me. In other words, I didn't run into a previous version of myself or create copies. This was good, because the world needed no more than one Oliver Twist.

I had, on rare occasion, brought along someone with me. So, I knew that my plan *might* work. I was going to try and transport the three of us back, moments in time. If we stayed here, the Zulus would outflank us. If we moved, Stinger would cut us down. Our only chance was to find a more manageable position. We knew where the Zulus had first fired, so the plan was to head in the opposite direction – assuming the rules of my timepiece allowed it.

Of course, what was a rule that wasn't worth breaking? This would certainly bend those boundaries. Pushing those thoughts to the side, I set about the task at hand telling them, "We need to huddle tight if this is going to work."

After a moment of awkward shuffling, Pip and Stella found themselves close to each other. Remarkably close. The scent of vanilla and rose perfume arose from Stella, cutting through sweat and dust for a moment as we huddled in tightly. "With any luck, we'll end up back on the path by the Palace, before the Zulus open fire."

"But this time with a plan," Pip said.

"Oh!" Stella's eyes widened as if what we'd said in all this craziness finally made sense. "Like a respawn point in *Dark Souls*?"

"Sure, whatever that is." My inability to communicate with Stella didn't seem to cut both ways. Nothing I said seemed to confuse her for long.

And for Pip, well, Stella could have told him that the moon was one giant scone and Pip would have provided her with a spot o' tea.

Someone yelled out an order and the gatling gun greeted us with another hail of bullets. Shrapnel of brick dust spat at us. "Time to go." I pointed to a clump of trees whose bark hadn't been pockmarked by bullet holes and spears. "We make a break into the treeline, then across the street into the back alleys following the trail of blood to our dinosaur. Keep the warriors trailing us, but not too much. Those stubby, stabbing spears are as dangerous in close quarters as the gatling gun is to us in the open."

"No worries," Pip shouted over the noise, "If we get separated, pick up the trail of blood. If we lose that listen for—"

"The bloodcurdling screams?" Stella finished.

"Simple enough." Pip held Stella's hands as he reassured her. At first, she seemed unsure, as if surprised by the advance, but after a soft exchange of looks between the two, her hands settled within his.

The roar of the gatling gun stopped. There was silence but for the buzzing in my ears. Butts of spears beat on the cobblestones as the Zulus advanced on our position. I thumbed the pinion on my watch, which was habit, really. The Spirit of the Past, whoever had taken on that mantle moved me (and hopefully Pip and Stella) through time. All I did was will it. Still, I liked the idea of *doing* something instead of thinking it.

Spherical light surrounded us. My skin tingled as it always did. My heart raced faster, as if caught in a surge of electricity. Everything lifted upwards, as if we were magnets caught in a current. It felt prolonged this time, most likely because it was three of us jetting back to the past instead of little ol' me.

"Hello, Oliver."

That voice again. So familiar . . .

We screamed back to the past as I figured it out.

"Nell?"

I stood there, dazed. Surely, Nell had passed, I had seen her spirit ascend beyond our realm. How?

Pip pushed me forward. "Don't stand around mate," he yelled. "This was your plan, now run." Pip and Stella raced off, together. They looked back at me, fear on their face as a spear rushed past mine. "Go!"

Through the trees, I ran, pumping my legs as a fury of shouts rose behind me and the recollection of Nell's soft-spoken voice stuck in my mind. I twisted through the elms, oaks, and London plane trees of Hyde Park as a spear sliced through the air, striking a spruce. The end of the weapon vibrated as the blade sunk deeply into the bark. Pip and Stella remained unharmed as we cut across the tree line from Hyde Park into the city.

I followed the trail of blood and found myself on South Carriage, heading toward the grounds of Buckingham and the Thames beyond. London was not the bustling slice of city life it usually was. Random acts of time slippage had kept people shuttered indoors.

That was good news for us as it meant less collateral damage. But it also meant that the missing array of costermonger carts and carriages clogging cobblestone streets gave us little to hide behind as the Zulu warriors hunted us down.

What had we done to piss them off? It remained a mystery, but I thought it had something to do with being thrown around in time, something I could occasionally relate to. But you know who *would* know? Nell.

She was a warm redhead tinkerer who was always ten steps ahead before I'd even figured out the game. Her radiant smile cut through grey clouds. And the fierceness in her eyes when you'd spent a considerable amount of effort in getting her angry, as her murderer had done, commanded respect. I wondered—

A spear shot passed my ear and stuck inside the mortar between two bricks at a savings bank I'd raced by. The alleyway beside it seemed forever out of reach and so it would be if one of those spears had found its target.

Another spear flashed by where my chest had been. I had to reach the maze of alleyways before I was made into a human pincushion.

Finally, the alley opened. Or should I say, closed in? Narrow, dim alleyways in London were notorious places for violence and sewage and homelessness. Normally, that would deter anyone from seeking these darkened dens as a place for refuge. For me, they were a haven. I blew my breath out, stopping for a moment to collect myself. I didn't have long before the gatling gun found me and fired. Brick exploded above my head. Damn, these warriors were persistent.

Three of them, all barefoot and bare-chested, had determined looks in their eyes as if I had done something to personally offend them. They swarmed me, their wide, sword-like spears pointing menacingly. Looking ahead, I'd lost sight of Pip and Stella. I didn't know where to go or what to do. My heart thumped so loudly I swore I could hear it echo through the alley.

A door to my right opened and Pip's hand grabbed my arm. He jerked me inside and slammed the door shut. Pip and I shoved a solid oak case to barricade it. "You all right, Oliver?" Pip asked, pushing the heavy shelf against the entrance. "You look like you saw a ghost."

I had seen ghosts before. But just now, it had been a voice. She'd called my name. It had to have been her. I said as much to the others, "Nell."

"I'm sorry, mate, I haven't the foggiest who she is. Can she help us?"

I shook my head. "I don't know."

Thudding came from the other side. Our makeshift fortress wouldn't hold for long. The wall behind us was connected to a long row of buildings, affording us a few minutes to prepare before our pursuers looped around the alleyway and caught us or they broke through the door.

"They seem a determined lot," Pip said.

"They probably think it's our fault that they're here," Stella replied.

"Is there another way out?"

Stella pointed to the other side of the shop. Where there should have been a wall, or a window was a ruin of brick, wood, and glass. Emptiness opened the shop to the street beyond, obscured by shadows and fog.

It took a moment for my eyes to adjust to the darkened room before chaos came into clarity. But it was the scent of the place that told me where I was even before I saw all the blood. Foggy, grey sunlight lit the far side of the room by way of the missing wall, proved my assumption.

"That's not what I think?" Stella gagged. I didn't blame her. The copper metallic smell was nauseating. "This wasn't a person?"

"No," I answered, pointing to a row of empty meat hooks hanging from the ceiling. There was a space where a hook was missing. I found it on the floor, mangled. Ahead, a counter full of small pieces of raw chicken, goose, and pig, lay bloodied and scattered on the floor, the slivers of meat too tiny to eat, I guess. But the big cow carcasses that had once hung on these hooks here were all gone.

"The butcher's shop." Pip said. "Thank heavens."

I agreed. Our dinosaur had found a meal. And while he had made a gruesome mess, it wasn't a crime scene. Maybe full, our dinosaur might be a tad happier, I hoped.

"I think I'm going to be sick," Stella said. She went off to the corner of the store and hunched over while Pip and I maintained our position against the door. The pounding against it stopped, which must have meant that the Zulus were rushing through the alleyway to get to us. Or it was a feint to draw us out. Military strategy had always been beyond me. I'd charge forward, second-guess myself mid-stride, mess up, and use my watch to fix it all. It was the only plan I needed.

"We can't stay here," I instructed the others. I hoped I was right.

"Only way out is ahead," Pip urged. Besides, the plan was to introduce the Zulus to our dinosaur, or, as I liked to call it: the worst blind date ever.

The color in Stella's face returned as we regrouped. We ran through the remains of the butcher shop and out onto the street. Caution was for chumps. As we bolted out, the door cracked open, and three Zulus piled in after us. So, it had been a feint; luckily for us, we hadn't fallen for it. I wonder what they would make of all that blood. Respect? We knew what had done it. They did not. It occurred to me that the Zulus might join forces with our dinosaur against us, combining to form, what? MegaZulusauruses?

Outside, we were wedged into a thin strip of street surrounded by a long, unbroken row of shops on either side except for a narrow, dark alley on the opposite side of the street. As I suspected, ahead on the main thoroughfare was our dinosaur, its reddish-black featherlike features ruffled in the breeze, and fresh blood dripped from its teeth. We'd found our quarry, but I hadn't wanted to find it *this* close.

"Other way," I said. The three of us retraced our steps only to face the main bulk of the Zulu warriors with the gatling gun. "Back inside!"

But the three warriors who had splintered the door were already on us, spears poised to strike. The dinosaur turned at our noise, its eyes sizing us as easy prey. The three of us pressed our backs together, surrounded by enemies.

"Wait," I said. "This wasn't part of the plan."

Chapter 10
A Sliver of Hope

My head spun as I raced through our options. A quick scan of the street showed a narrow alleyway, but it was too far away and likely led to a dead end. The shops here were tightly packed, their weathered brick storefronts made for a continuous wall down the cobblestone street. Wooden shingled roofs sloped to either side, as if each of the buildings were leaning on their neighbors for support. Gaslamps lit the interiors of shops – grocers, fabric, and homewares – while clotheslines crossed overhead from the second-floor residences, trapping us in a foggy, dim artery of London somewhere north of the Thames and west of Piccadilly Circus.

The Zulus had been poised to strike with two lines of warriors extending out on both sides of their formation, like horns. A giant of a man stood in the middle, likely this groups' war chief, and a man with designs in white chalk all over his skin stood beside him. I think he was the one who had earlier spoken English. He kept them from attacking us, for now. I think the dinosaur had given them pause. They eased off a little at the sight of the fearsome creature.

The dinosaur had freshly eaten. That was likely the only reason it hadn't attacked yet. I had the feeling that it was behaving defensively and if we didn't provoke it further, it wouldn't harm us. However, I wasn't willing to test that theory out with our lives just yet.

The beast took a measured step forward, as if deciding to fight or to flee. Maybe it really was looking for a way out of this and it just wanted to be left alone.

"It was heading toward the water, Oliver." The voice again. Nell. It came from my pocket watch, there was no mistaking it this time. "She's thirsty and tired. She's scared and looking for a way out."

Pip and Stella snapped their heads at the voice. Pip asked, "Is your watch, uh, talking?"

I nodded. "Nell, I need a plan before we become a *Barber of Fleet Street* special."

"You have everything you need to solve your predicament," Nell said. Some help she was. Puzzling as ever.

The creature could retreat down the street. It was empty. But that meant turning its back on us. It seemed to shrink back as if headed in that direction while keeping an eye on us. We could follow it, keep people safe, and find a place to corral it. This was going to work—

A shop's bell chimed. At any other moment, the small little jingle would have been lost among the hustle and bustle of the busy street. Now, it seemed as out of place as a dinosaur stalking the streets of London.

Oh, right.

The bell brought the beast's attention to the shop. A father and his daughter stepped onto the cobblestones away from the relative safety of a bakery, oblivious to the mess they'd stumbled into. The girl was the first to notice. Her scream swiveled her father's head to the scene. The dinosaur swung around to face them, its tail swooshing above our heads at break-neck speed.

Its escape path was now cut-off, the dinosaur was trapped. And cornered creatures were never friendly.

"Now what do we do?" Pip asked.

"Looks like not everyone got the memo to stay inside," Stella said. I had no idea what a memo was, but I understood the context. The father and daughter both carried thick loaves of bread under each arm. They wore rags and the father had no shoes. I realized that they weren't shoppers but were instead hungry and homeless. Bread thieves yes, but when you saw an opportunity not to starve you had to take it. I could relate, no matter how poor an idea. Oh, I could relate to bad decisions too. Like what I was about to do.

"Time to ask for the Zulus' help. Especially if we're going to save those people," I gulped.

"Right, they're not likely to kill you the moment you speak up," Pip said cynically. "But if you do manage to not die, put in a good word for me, won't you, chap? They still have Stinger. I'd like to return it unharmed."

I half ignored Pip as I placed my pocket watch in his hand, my eyes locking with his: "Hold this for me. You might need this for what I'm about to ask you to do."

"Wait, you're trusting me with your watch?" he asked.

"I'm trusting you with our lives."

"Is that all?"

Oh, this was probably a mistake. "I need you and Stella to rescue that family while I try to talk our way out of this with the Zulus, and maybe get them on our side." Pip's pale face went a shade paler.

"You want us to get closer to that thing?" Stella asked, in dramatic fashion, as if she were in a stage play.

"Pip has my watch should you run into trouble."

She gulped and her shoulders slumped.

"At least with Stinger," Pip said, "we could have maintained our distance."

"With any luck, the Zulus will help."

"That's a lot of luck."

I clutched my cane tightly with the knowledge that my wits and weapons would be useless against a dozen battle-hardened warriors should things go poorly. Pip and Stella crept toward the father and his daughter and away from the Zulus, who didn't hinder their leaving.

I believe I picked up a few modern obscenities from Stella, some words being more universal than others. The dinosaur eyed them suspiciously, unsure of what to do.

"We don't have much time," I said, addressing the fierce warrior in the center who I hoped was the leader. He stared me down, but he did not kill me outright. Progress. I pointed to my friends and to the family in the street "Can you help me? Help us save the girl and her father?"

There was nothing but silence from their leader as his followers eyed me, pointing their weapons at my heart. I gulped hard, hoping that Pip could use the watch to save me from myself if he didn't need it for Stella or himself first. But I was here now, I might as well commit. I didn't know how to communicate with them, so I pantomimed throwing a spear at the dinosaur. I jerked my empty arms out and toward the creature, surely looking like a jester at court.

"What are you doing?" A wiry man with unfamiliar designs in white clay over his face and chest approached from behind the chieftain. I thought he might be an advisor. He looked me over. "We do not throw our *iklwa*. Are you a fool?"

"Sometimes. You speak English?"

"It was the language forced on me in the Missions by our oppressors. *You.*" He stabbed a finger at me. Fortunately, it was his hand, not his sharp *iklwa,* that he'd used. "Your people spill our blood onto our lands."

Oh. I realized why they were quick to shoot at us. "I'm sorry, I understand your anger, but I am not your enemy, I'm not even from your time. But people here, right now, are going to get hurt by that creature. Will you help us?"

"Who are they?" The Zulu asked. "The father and his daughter? What do they mean to you?"

"They're people who need our help."

The Megalosaurus saw Pip and Stella as nothing more than flies. It swung its massive head back and forth, as if trying to swat the two away while they tried in vain to reach the pair who'd become frozen with fear.

The dinosaur attacked. It darted the remaining steps to the family and puffed out its feathers, opened its jaws and lunged.

The Zulu chief shouted an order. At once every Zulu that I saw, including the three on our side, snapped to attention, the butts of fifteen spears striking the cobblestone at the same exact second. Their sound stopped the dinosaur.

A long spear, longer than the shorter *iklwa*, whistled past my ear. The lone spear struck the creature. I was sad that it had to end this way. But it was for the best.

Oh.

The spear fell harmlessly off the creature and clattered to the ground. I'd seen those same spears lodged into the mortar between bricks. *How?*

Another long spear flew from the Zulu formation. But the beast had turned its attention on its attacker and was now lumbering toward us, each step bringing its teeth and girth inexorably closer to our squishy, fragile bodies. The second spear proved to be no more helpful than the first, striking it where its feathered and leathered skin offered protection from our weapons. One should always remember – don't bring pointy sticks to a dinosaur fight.

I remembered, of course, that the Zulus hadn't just brought sticks. They'd brought Stinger. With a roar of its own, the gatling gun burst into action, aiming high to avoid hitting our allies down the street.

Even with warning, the exploding gunpowder sent me turning and ducking, hands pressed against my ears. At the sound of the gun, the dinosaur broke off its charge entirely and . . . disappeared?

The Zulus had overshot, and the dinosaur had lunged low. Gunsmoke created a cloudy bank of grey that had mingled and married with the coal-dark fog. This had allowed the dinosaur to flee into the narrow side-alley I'd spotted earlier; as a possible escape for us. Apparently, the alley was wide enough for the creature to squeeze through, something I didn't think possible.

With the gatling gun silenced, I could hear my thoughts once more. *Good plan, Twist, solid. Lost it – again.* How do you lose a fifteen foot, two-storey high dinosaur?

The Zulu chief spoke a new command and the Zulus broke into a chant. I had expected cheers, for vanquishing their foe, but instead, it was a low, slow melody, that suggested mourning. The song was beautiful, almost hymnal. It was poetry that could cut your soul more sharply than a sword.

No one had been killed. The father and daughter duo had quickly fled to safety once Pip and Stella had restored some sense to them. So, I didn't understand why the sad song. With that, he snapped an order again, the song silenced, and the Zulus once again tightened into a defensive formation.

"We regret that we must kill such a brave creature," the man in the white chalk told me. He introduced himself as Mandla and his chief as Solomon, like the biblical King. I suppose that influence had been our doing.

"We don't want the dinosaur dead," I furrowed my brow. In that moment, I had decided that our dinosaur was a girl, and it should live, if possible. I was starting to root for it. Her.

"You are unwise," Mandla said. I wasn't going to win 'British Man of the Year' with him. "However, the creature is a brave and formidable opponent. It deserves honor."

"Well, it fled," Pip said, returning from down the street with Stella. "It's quiet."

"Don't you know never to say that?" Stella wiped her eyes, the acrid smoke hung heavily. I could hardly see through my own watering eyes. "Something always happens the moment anyone ever says that."

We all waited expectantly for a moment. Nothing happened.

"I've been wrong from time to time," she said. The Zulus, for their part, remained ready.

"Back to square one, are we?" Pip's voice became clear after I rubbed a finger in my ears. Something ticked at the back of my brain. Something

Nell had said earlier about the creature being scared. "I think we're going about this the wrong way. We can use this time to come up with a new plan."

"You better take this, ol' boy." Pip held my watch out to me, ready to return it.

The ground shook. A low percussion punched through my chest, like standing too close to a drummer. Pip pocketed the watch. "I thought it left?"

"I take it back," Stella said, "I hate being right all the time."

Directly in front of us, through the deep dark fog and smoke hiding the creature, a toothy snout appeared . . .

Chapter 11
Rampage

The dinosaur emerged enraged, charging out from the fog on a warpath toward the gun. She barreled into the barrel of the weapon, dislodging it from the wooden undercarriage. The support structure burst into splinters while the iron cylinder thudded heavily onto the street. Stinger had stung its last.

The mighty Megalosaurus pressed its frenzied advantage by bowling into the wall of hardened Zulus. They broke, as they were shoved by the dinosaur, collapsing into each other in a cascade of falling dominoes that rippled out to us. Pip, Stella, and I were knocked onto the cold cobblestones. I landed hard on my side.

From my prone position, the dinosaur appeared impossibly large. She stood with her foot firmly on the gatling gun's barrel, crushing it, and letting forth another powerful growl that made my ears ring and my chest shake.

Victory in hand, the now bloodthirsty creature switched from prey to predator. Eyeing Pip, who rose onto his wobbling feet, she looked over her next meal the way one might drool over a table set with a Christmas feast.

A bead of sweat rolled down Pip's brow. The creature stared him down. Pip had my watch. If he became lunch, there was nothing I could do, I couldn't save him. He shot me a questioning look.

Run.

But where? Any direction he moved was within easy striking distance, like standing in front of a viper ready to pounce.

The dinosaur dove down, jaws wide, saliva and blood dripping. Pip's arms were raised in a futile defensive gesture.

The dinosaur's jaws clamped down—

On air.

Stella dove into Pip, pushing him back onto the ground and rolling over with him. The two recovered quickly, with only a moment's glance into each other's eyes. The butt of a short spear slammed into the side of the creature's face, momentarily stunning her and buying Pip and Stella time to retreat. They hobbled away, arm-in-arm, frantic and breathing hard.

Stella stood in front of Pip, pressing them both toward the street's edge. The Zulus struggled to regroup, and I stood, now the closest one to the dinosaur's maw, meaning I was on top of her menu. Maybe I could walk slowly away . . .

Nope. Her attention darted toward me. The creature, now flanked on all sides, stretched out, whipping her feathery tail, opening her jaw wide with rage. She let out a bone-chilling bellow.

The creature hadn't run away earlier. Instead, she had regrouped, come up with a plan, and had ripped into us like Pip's cab driver on a bustling street.

But now, her momentum waned, and her anger, which at first had been channeled into her cunning attack, had now once again become fueled by fear.

Wait. Isn't that what Nell had mentioned? Something about being lost, thirsty, and scared? I needed my watch.

Our stand-off was interrupted by a staccato mechanical rumble from down the street, increasing in volume as it roared closer.

"Oliver, you have any other magical powers that we don't know about?" Pip asked.

"Uh," I couldn't think of anything until I recognized that motor a moment later. I smiled, relaxing my shoulders and stiffening my spine "Just the magic of friendship."

Pip groaned again. His displeasure was cut off as the mechanical rumbling caught everyone's attention. Pip and Solomon turned looks of disbelief, as if the motor was stranger than a dinosaur displaced from time. Speaking of, she snapped randomly at us, rearing from the sound. She growled, her feather-like quills poised high, puffed up to make herself look larger.

Soon, a two-wheeled contraption emerged from the fog with a familiar face riding atop. Was that the steam-cycle I'd begged Dodger to build? Handy.

Lifting her goggles up, Dodger came to a stop, the engine idling, smoke chugging out the back pipes. "Ollie, hop on. Can you get that dinosaur's attention?"

"You built this?" It wasn't as refined as the one Nell had built in an alternate timeline, but it ran. It ran despite being a rusted and bluish, bone-breaker bicycle frame that had been Frankensteined together with an engine. The steam-power motor was welded and geared to a set of chains on the back wheel. And several smokestacks arose from behind an uncomfortable looking seat. I recovered my cane from the ground and hopped on because sure, why not? Between my two options, this one seemed safer, though not by much.

I thought I heard Stella say, "You built a motorcycle in the middle of the nineteenth century?" Though I could have sworn she said, "deathtrap" instead of "motorcycle".

As soon as I was on, Dodger peeled away.

"I have a plan." I aimed my cane above the dinosaur's head, letting the heavy brass ball fly as Nell had designed.

The dinosaur didn't like that at all, like she'd had this happen to her before. I didn't know how, but in any case, she flinched, like a dog dodging a kick from its master. I winced at that.

It reminded me that Nell had said, "She's scared." I needed to lead her away to safety and isolation. The blunt ball at the end of my cane was attached by a thin wire. As soon as it struck the ground, the dinosaur gave chase. I reeled back the ball and the creature joined us in pursuit as if we were a lure that she had to catch.

The steam-cycle sped up with a bang and puff of grey exhaust smoke. Wind whipped past my face bringing along with it wisps of Dodger's hair. She smelled of sweat and gin, her preferred perfume. I perched precariously behind her, one arm wrapped around her waist, holding tightly, while the dinosaur went after us.

We were a little slow to pick up speed. I looked up and she was there. Her jaw was within inches of us, her stench overpowering Dodger's day-old-gin. At least she was away from the others. It was the two of us versus an irate dinosaur – a typical weekend.

"Oliver if that thing eats me, I swear I will come back to haunt you, and not in the nice way like Nell." The steam-cycle picked up speed and we shot forward.

"Funny you should say that. Speaking of Nell, I think she wants us to head for the river."

"Nell said that?" Dodger's incredulity could be heard even over the noise of the engine. "Didn't she die?"

"Twice, I think. I've lost count." The heavy footfalls of the dinosaur shook the street, the steam-cycle wobbled but Dodger kept us balanced and ahead of sharp teeth. A turn was coming up ahead.

"We're going to talk about that later—"

"Turn right," I told her.

"Where?" Dodger sped past the intersection.

"There."

"You have to tell me to turn before the turn."

"I did," I yelled. The missed turn would have widened the gap between us and our angry pursuer. Instead, the dinosaur's hot breath froze the hairs on the back of my neck.

"Head toward the Thames."

"I know, you said that. But that turn isn't the quickest way to the river."

"It's not?"

"This is." She eschewed my directions and continued straight. Ahead, the road ended at a T-intersection, splitting off into the direction of a church and a row of pubs on the left and a residential area on the right. Neither was a great place for a rampaging dinosaur.

A fun fact about London, or any large city, was that an empty space never stayed empty for long. A row of costermonger carts had built up at the end of our street. They were hawking pippins and meat pies in peace until we arrived with our rather large and toothy companion.

Behind them was a grassy rise that fell into a steep incline. It was the embankment of the Thames. That's where our road ended. Unfortunately, it was exactly where we needed to go. But we couldn't go straight, not through the—

"Dodger, we're not going that way," Dodger liked to dodge things; this was plowing straight through. "Are we?"

"Hold on."

We were.

The pit in my stomach hardened as we plowed through the carts piled high with pippins of yellow and red. They flew into the air as if they were thrown by a drunken juggler. Two poor blokes and a lady hawking their goods gave us angry looks as their carts overturned, their wares ruined. The lady shouted profanities at us that would make milk curdle.

A shorter man in a faded flat cap and worn threads fled, not only knocking over his own cart, but also his neighbor's. Another cart exploded into toothpicks as our toothy, grinning friend crashed through it. I didn't see where the sellers went, but our dinosaur didn't stop to chow down. I presumed they'd fled to safety though I couldn't say the same thing for the stalls that were now fit for firewood.

"You think Pip will pay for that?" I clutched Dodger tightly.

"Pip is part of the problem," Dodger disagreed.

A flat panel from a cart had fallen into an upward angle. It made for a hastily improvised ramp that bridged the street to the grassy knoll ahead.

We shot up it and into the air. There was a moment of weightlessness as we lost our seating. Dodger held onto the handles, and I held onto her.

I looked back to see eye to eye with our pursuer to find that we were at convenient biting height. With a quick snap of her neck her jaws flanked me for a long, solitary second. Rotting flesh stung my nose. I didn't want to be eaten by a dinosaur, I imagined the dagger-like teeth ripping me apart, writhing in pain until my body finally gave out. I hoped it would be over quickly.

"Did you have to go this way?"

"It's the scenic route." Some scenery. It was the inside of a dinosaur's jaws. Dark and smelly, though I have to say that there were a few slums I've slept in as a child that matched this description.

Gravity aided my near-miss as the dinosaur's dinner. We dropped below its snapping jaws as they clamped down on air. The steam-cycle plummeted downward into nothingness. I looked to see the dinosaur cock her head sidewise to eye us angrily.

Dodger landed the steam-cycle with a rough thump as we both slammed back into the seat. Note to self: add cushioning. We were on a wide granite gravel road that demarcated the warehouse district along this leg of the Thames. The bank of the river loomed ahead, while piers, wharfs, and large and mostly empty buildings sat awaiting their wares.

We neared the edge of the river as our Megalosaurus crested the hill overlooking the Thames and us. As soon as she saw the water, she stopped and shook her feathery head. I didn't know what that meant, but I could sense an immediate change in the creature's demeanor. It darted off along the edge of the embankment like a puppy looking for a way down.

"You can stop squeezing me so tightly now." Dodger loosened my vise-like grip around her waist. My hands were stiff and white-knuckled. Dodger's coat was wrinkled and damp from sweat where my arms had been.

Later, I would realize that if I had paid more attention, I would have noticed that she didn't say to stop holding her, only to loosen my grip. Does everyone replay conversations in their head? Just me?

"Oh, sorry," I mumbled absently as the steam-cycle slid from a spin into a stop. I hardly heard her. Instead, all I could hear was the thump of my own chest and the thrum of the steam-cycle. I shouldn't have been so shaken, strange days like these were becoming routine.

The dinosaur had eased her way down, completely ignoring us as it passed. A fisherman quietly reeled in his catch, gathered his tackle and hurried off as she stooped low beside him, stretched out a tongue and began lapping the water feverishly.

Around us large, sagging, dilapidated wooden structures dotted the river edge like a sparse cowboy town in the American west. This area was mostly abandoned as the rebuilt steam-works moved many of the jobs and factories upriver. London's warehouses and wharfs were centralized either there or on the Isle of Dogs, both miles away from our current location, directly south and some ways from Hyde Park. It was one of the few quiet places in the city, for the moment, until some wide-eyed entrepreneur gobbled it up to build low-wage, rat-infested blacking factories.

As we caught our breath, Dodger cut off the engine. The dinosaur took a long moment to consider us. With a shake of her head, she wandered off, deciding we were no longer worth her time. The ground shook as she stomped away, and a cloud of rock dust kicked up in her wake.

We watched as she found herself a cool patch of shade within the walls of a warehouse that had its giant doors open. There was a flock of pigeons roosting on the grounds. They stood there quizzically, cooing, until she rushed them. They flapped away skittishly, surrendering their home to the larger bird-like creature.

She turned around several times, tucked in her feathery tail, and nestled into a ball and closed her eyes. In seconds, or what seemed like seconds, the creature emitted what I could only describe as a snore. Nell had been right. She needed safety and a place to quench her thirst. Everything I needed was right in front of me. I never needed to run off with Pip.

"Is that thing . . . asleep?" Dodger asked.

"Let's hope so. Because we need to close those doors."

"Go right ahead, Ollie, I'll wait here."

"Right," I stuttered sheepishly. "I don't have my watch if that thing wakes up."

"Be very quiet."

Shutting her inside the derelict structure wouldn't contain her if she wanted out. But it might offer some privacy and keep people from poking sticks at her. Plus, it might buy us time to come up with a real solution. "What we need to do is regroup with the others and figure out how to get this thing back to its own time."

"You still need Pip's help?" Dodger's delivery was cold but correct. "Let me have one guess where your watch is."

If I didn't know better, I'd think she was jealous. But it wasn't just that. She was right, I shouldn't have run off with Pip and left her and the children in danger. Nor should I have given him my watch. I knew that now. And if there was also some jealousy there, I wondered how she would handle Nell being back in the equation.

"Not just Pip. We picked up another time-traveler," I offered freely. "And the Zulus, who we need to keep on our side."

"I saw them," she said. "Anyone else?"

I didn't answer. She already knew.

"I thought so."

"We need answers, Nell has them."

Dodger wordlessly started up the steam-cycle. I worried that it would wake the dinosaur, but it remained firm in its slumber as I closed and secured both doors without incident.

Back on the steam-cycle together, we raced off, my arms not so tightly around Dodger this time, as if the space between us had grown icy.

All the while, I continued to wonder what Dodger would make of things now that Nell was back. Well, sort of, if you counted a disembodied voice stuck in a watch as being back. Today was already crazy enough with Pip coming between Dodger and I and whatever time-travel shenanigans were going on without relationships complicating things. Now, the two ladies I had feelings for and who both liked me were thrown back into the mix. How would it all work out?

Time would tell.

Chapter 12
At the Brink

The fog was clearing as Dodger and I roared back on the steam-cycle to Pip, Stella, and the Zulus. They were joined by Bucket and his men, and they all appeared to be in some sort of stand-off. So much for a quiet break.

Spring sun shone off the copper buttons of the Inspector's immaculate uniform. He had returned with a frenzy of Peelers, nightsticks out and ready in combative stances.

Dodger cut off the cycle's steam-engine. I dismounted quickly as it spasmed to a stop, like a possessed demon. Dodger and I needed to talk. But now was not the time.

I had also wanted to ground my feet onto good ol' *terra firma*. While the cycle was speedy, safe it was not. But enough about my worries, Dodger and I had returned safely, and our Big Beasty was safely snoring away in a storehouse along the Thames. So, I was surprised to see Bucket's bobbies on-edge. You turn your back one moment . . . There simply wasn't enough of me to keep an eye on the entire city. Maybe Pip could arrange franchise opportunities?

"It's not safe for you here," Bucket said on our approach.

"We just had a big monster with long, sharp teeth try to eat us." Dodger poked a finger at his shiny buttons. She was always trying to provoke the police. Or anyone with authority for that matter. But she was getting better. She hadn't outright punched him. Yet. "I think we'll be fine."

Dodger turned to face me, unleashing a slap across my face. "No thanks to you."

"What was that for?" I rubbed my cheek gingerly. It stung. The Inspector stared at her, probably thankful that she hadn't done the same to him. I think Dodger had some anger issues. But she was right – I deserved her ire. And handprint. A stinging handprint right across the face.

"You," Dodger said with her voice rising, "got Edward hurt. Byron has scrapes and cuts all over. Abbey was scared. You failed them."

"I'm . . ." I continued rubbing my cheek, looking to Bucket for backup. What hurt more than the slap was the truth.

"She's got a point, son." Bucket coughed, jerking our attention to the road ahead. "I hate to break up your squabble, but we have a situation. There's a contingent of Africans armed with dangerous weapons. I need you and everyone to keep back until we can subdue them and clear the area."

"Oh, the Zulus?" I asked. "They're the good guys." *I hoped.*

What was Dodger saying about the foundlings? They were safe for now, I knew, otherwise Dodger wouldn't have left them to go save my bacon.

However, there were more immediate concerns. I'd barely managed a truce with the warriors. Bucket's men looked as if they were about to start a war. Now what had the Inspector gone and done?

"Of course, they're with you." Bucket took off his uniform hat and shook his head. "Things like this never used to happen before you went heroic. London has never been a peaceful city, but it never spontaneously blew up or spawned spirits."

"Just an unhappy coincidence." I gulped down the lie. I could hear the ruckus ahead. The Zulus had started one of their chants. It sounded like their first chant after they confronted the dinosaur. I knew what that meant. This might have been all my fault, but it could grow deadly if I didn't diffuse the situation between the Zulus and the Peelers.

I pushed past the Inspector despite his protestations. Dodger was at my side, but I could feel her eyes needle into me as she warned, "You and me? We're not done yet. We need to talk."

There was warmth in her words. I don't think she would have been so angry with me if she didn't care. However, I didn't relish the idea of being chewed out by Dodger later. I had been hoping to ask her to dinner, not be served up to her on a platter.

***

Pip and Stella's backs were against each other, each trying to stem the anger of their respective groups of armed and agitated men. Neither noticed us as we regrouped. Stella was too busy pushing back the Zulus, while Pip parlayed the Peelers.

For each of the dozen Zulu warriors, there stood in opposition to them a Peeler. But the Zulus were in ordered formation, chanting their song of superiority in battle. The Peelers may have worn uniforms, but that was the only thing uniform about them. They were an angry mob of wooden truncheons. I wasn't a betting man, but in this case, I could make a safe bet who would win if these two sides came to blows.

When I tapped Pip on his shoulder, he shot me a look of relief.

"We asked for *dinosaurs versus robots*," he said. He blocked an encroaching Peeler, only to have another wag his truncheon at an unflinching Zulu. "This isn't that."

"Where's our translator, Where's Mandla?" I asked as loud as my voice would carry.

"I've talked to him, but he's waiting for you. He said you lied to him." Oh.

Mandla, stepped out from the ranks of warriors. He looked weary. "We want to go home."

From behind, Bucket said, "I'd like 'em all to go home too."

"They don't have a home, Inspector," I tried to explain, "They were brought here against their will. Just like the creature."

"But they're standing here, holding spears out on the street." Bucket protested. "Could be a danger."

"Could be?" Dodger asked, her voice stretching the first word out an octave "Standing around?"

"With weapons," Bucket said. "They should stop resisting."

"Your Peeler's provocations aren't helping, Chief," Pip said. "Trust in Twist. We're supposed to be partnering with him."

"Inspector, tell your men to stand down."

"It's not a good idea," he said. I wasn't sure if he was going to listen to me. Nevertheless, he placed his cover back onto his head. For a uniformed man, that was a promising start that a decision was being made.

"Here's an idea," Dodger said. "Why don't you take your men on a trek down by the river?"

Bucket bunched his mustache.

I stepped in to explain: "Our feathery, sharp-toothed friend from earlier is there."

"Oh? What's your point?"

"She's a larger threat than these blokes here," Dodger offered sarcastically. "Though she's sweeter than you imbeciles."

"She did seem kinda sweet if you could get to know her," Stella said from against a wall of warriors. "You know, instead of being eaten."

"Right now, our beasty is quiet. She's sleeping off the stock of a butcher's shop and is quite content inside a warehouse." I explained further and told them which building to look for. "If you don't get your men down there to evacuate the area and blockade the streets, there's going to be a lot more to worry about than my friends here when she wakes up hungry again. These Zulus are under my protection. You protect the civilians down by the Thames. Everyone wins. Order your men to stand down, please."

Bucket responded by mulling it over. See? Politeness never hurt.

"That means now, ya' bloody Bobby." Dodger said.

Or not.

Meanwhile, a young Zulu looked as if to break ranks, his spear within easy reach of a Peeler's heart. That only angered the mob more. If Bucket didn't break this up now, it would be too late. Words would spill into blood.

The Inspector's face turned red. He might have hated how we spoke to him, hated that we were right, hated that he didn't have control of the situation himself, but he was a good man. He didn't have the full picture that I possessed. Nevertheless, he was intelligent, humble, and wary of the world around him. After a few years under Scrooge's thumb, I think he was finally starting to come into his own. I thought of Bucket as a match to the young, upstart detective that lived off Baker Street. That guy, I disliked.

"Men," he snapped with the gusto of a stern schoolmaster. The Peeler's protests quieted though they weren't outright quelled. The Zulus stopped chanting even though they were under no such direction to do so. "We move south, toward the Thames. We have, uh, an even bigger threat to public safety that must be dealt with accordingly."

Bucket's men growled and grumbled at the order. Clearly, they thought the direction daft. But it *was* an order and so they reluctantly obeyed, trickling away from the scene like a leaky faucet. Finally, the last of the blue and white uniformed Peelers streamed to the waterfront.

"Thank you," Mandla said. I didn't think he was entirely grateful. They seemed to be itching for a fight. We denied them that.

"Well, that's two down," Pip said, brushing himself off. "One monster away and one bloody brawl avoided. But I'm afraid this frock coat is positively ruined, and Stinger is destroyed. Is this a typical day for you, Oliver?"

I nodded and took note of Stella, our other time-traveler. She'd been pressed in between Pip's back and the sharp spears of the Zulus for some time. Her clothes and hair were disheveled, and parts of her jacket had been ripped but she didn't seem as bothered.

"Are you all right?" I asked.

"I was up against a wall of shirtless, muscled men," she answered as if her hand was caught in the cookie jar, or *on* the cookie jar in this case. "I think I'll be okay."

I didn't know how to answer that, but Pip frowned.

"Speaking of our new friends," Dodger steered back to the topic at hand, "what do we do with them?"

"Let's let them decide," I said. "At least until we figure out what's going on and how we can help them home."

Solomon stepped forward, as did Mandla. The chief asked us something in his language. He went silent, nodding as his words were translated. Some of his body language was universal.

"Have you discovered what brought us here and more importantly, how we may return?" Mandla asked. "Why are we in the land of our enemy?"

I hoped he didn't think I was his enemy any longer. I didn't want to be on the wrong side of his spear. I also didn't have an answer for him, but I wasn't willing to let him know that yet. "What do you remember?"

"We were on a hunt in our lands," Mandla's white chalk patterns danced as he spoke. I found it mesmerizing as I hung on every word. "Our chief told us of great battles against soldiers of a far-away pale nation." That would be us, I noted. "And of many wars and victories to come. Our hearts yearned for this; such was our excitement." He went silent for a long moment before gesturing to his surroundings. "Then we found ourselves here. We thought it was an answer to our desires. Though we are few, we will fight you until there is no breath left for us to thrust our spear."

"No, no, you don't have to do that," Pip interjected.

"You led us here where we were confronted by the Great Beast, a worthy adversary," he said, "and we protected an innocent father and child." Mandla looked to his chief as if unsure how to continue. "We are unaccustomed to not knowing the path forward from this moment."

Welcome to the club.

"I can help with that." The voice came from Pip's pocket. He crinkled his brow for a moment before understanding struck him. "The watch." Pip pulled it out but guarded it close and tight, as if it were a silk handkerchief among a street full of shifty irregulars. "I forgot I had it. This must be Nell?"

It was.

"Oliver," she said, "You and your friends are quickly running out of time."

Chapter 13
Revelations

My childhood friend, a tinkerer, and one who had lived and died (and died again) under tragic circumstances. I missed her. Her warmth, her smile, the way she pushed aside her red hair when she was lost in a project, tinkering away at her newest invention.

For the longest time, she was simply a spirit, trapped in her Curiosity Shop, but even though she had no Earthly anchor, she became mine. Then, she was gone. And I hadn't gone an hour without her in my thoughts. But how had she returned and what did that mean?

"Nell," Dodger said, running to the watch and peering down into its face while hers brightened. "I've missed you!" Strange side of Dodger I was seeing. Considering when they first met, Dodger had tried to kill Nell, I'd say this reunion was going well. Of course, Dodger *had* killed me once upon a time, and here I was caught between whether she'd like carnations or tulips for the dinner I hadn't yet asked her to.

Mandla, Dodger, Stella, and I huddled around Pip's outstretched hand as we hoped Nell could explain what was going on. Stella, I noticed, was eyeing the timepiece warily. Finally, something from my time that mystified her.

"Are you the Spirit of the Past?" I asked. I knew that the Spirits that guided my time-travels were not permanent, that they could be interchanged at will. But how did Nell end up as one? Is that what had brought her back in whatever state this was? I had more questions than time.

"I can't talk about it now," Nell answered. "For time's sake, the simplest answer is that the spirits have changed, some for good, some for . . ." Her voice trailed off before delivering a warning in a strong, strident voice, "Be careful, Oliver. Times have changed and I can't always protect you. There is one who weaves all."

Weaves? No, that wasn't ominous sounding at all. What did she mean by—

"You're running out of time," Nell said, interrupting my thoughts. "Because time itself is breaking."

"We gathered that, Love." Dodger took a swig from a glass flask she had hidden in her pocket. "With that Big Beasty rampaging around and all. Don't see many of their kind at the London Zoo. Time is broken, but what else is new?"

"I think I've seen these movies," Stella said. "My roommate made me watch them and aside from the first one, they're all bad. I keep telling her that's why I have no interest in Hollywood. I want to stick with plays. 'If it's not on the page, it's not on the stage,' is what my instructor says. Maybe writers should remember that?"

Did Stella just mention studying to be an actress? Even if she had, I didn't know what this had to do with our dinosaur. Maybe her nerves were rattled. But after all she had gone through, what did she have to be nervous over now?

Mandla tapped the butt of his spear on the ground.

"People," Pip directed, "we're being sidetracked. Apocalypses here are so normal for you lot, so I suppose it's routine?"

He wasn't wrong.

"Time is running out," Nell reiterated. "I am not in control of what's happening, Oliver. It's not your watch."

If this wasn't my doing (thankfully), it meant that . . .

"I'm of limited help," Nell continued. "That means that I cannot send your warrior friends home. They are stuck here until you stop this, Oliver, and they can choose to fight with you or against you in the battles to come. I cannot promise any of you that you'll make it out of this alive."

"That's a Tuesday for us," Dodger said. "What exactly can you tell us, Love? What do you know?"

"That you'll have to band together to have a chance of surviving this fight."

We didn't have a prayer.

Mandla rested his arms in thought. "A chance of battle, no promise of safety, or assurance that we are fighting for the right side?" He spoke to his chief for a moment and turned back to me when he was done.

"We're all in this together and I need your help," I said. "But the choice is yours."

"We will see." They left to confer with their fellow warriors. As he did, Pip piped up. "I don't think it's a good idea. Remember, they attacked us."

"They were plucked from the timeline. They were scared."

"Who's to say they won't side with whoever is doing this? The enemy of my enemy might be their friend," he argued.

"It's a chance we'll have to take." I loosened my waistcoat. The sun beat hotly on this spring afternoon. Soon, however, I knew it would cool and darkness would descend once more. It always did. It would be good to have allies in the fight ahead, like an army of candles against the approaching darkness. "Stella, Dodger, what do you think?"

Stella added, "Did anyone want to ask me if I want to fight? I mean, there's got to be a perfectly safe coffee shop around here, right?"

"Coffee shop?"

"Yes, it's the custom in the future," Stella explained. "'*Caffeinate and create,*' I always say. There's a small hole-in-the-wall a short distance from the dorms. I don't like the big chains."

"That sounds rather cozy," Pip said. "I'd like to go to one, if we survive this." He took a moment as if to reconsider his position. The thing I liked about Pip was that, confronted with new information, he was willing to change his stance. Of course, in this instance, it could also mean that he had a hidden agenda. In the hours we've spent together so far, I'd only seen the tip of the iceberg with him.

He went on to explain, "I don't trust them. From all appearances they have nothing. No fine things, no fancy degrees. Yet they are proud, noble, and seem more content than any man I've ever seen on the Moors, outside of my Uncle Joe. I never understood what made him so happy."

"This uncle," I prodded, "do you trust him? Maybe they have something in common."

"Aye." He nodded his head. "Maybe there's more to them that I don't understand. But I'll confess to being stupefied over the whole affair. Leave it to me to make acquaintance with you, Oliver, just as you're pulling us into another one of your mad escapades."

"I get that a lot." I answered. But more seriously, I said, "Someone told me once, that life is who your friends are."

Mandla returned after what seemed like a heated debate of his own. A lump formed in my throat, for his demeanor had changed. He seemed friendly before, now, the veins on his neck and temples protruded, his voice was lower, and he seemed not angry, but disappointed. In us.

"Your people view us as savages," he said. While we debated if we should trust them, they were wondering the same thing about us, only, they had less reason to. "You invade our homes, destroy our crops, force your faith on us. Are we inferior? We don't possess your finery and your machines and for that we are viewed as such. But that is your philosophy, not ours. I am because we are," he stressed. "That is what you fail to realize. Perhaps if you learned from us, you would better understand that time is short for a man."

"Well, you're right about that," Dodger said.

"Your philosophy," Stella said, as if understanding what Mandla had meant, "Is 'we' instead of 'me'?"

"That is it. Perhaps there is hope," he said. "For a man, time is short. For all men, time is timeless."

"*Humanity*," Stella coughed.

"We do not trust you," he continued, addressing me. "But this is our fight, too."

I gave him a nod of appreciation. Somehow, I went from an unwanted orphan to leader of a small band that had to stop the end of the world. Or, as Nell said, the end of time.

As if to emphasize this momentous moment, the ground began shaking. We all widened our stances and looked around feverishly. The brick buildings lining our street trembled along with us, but nothing appeared to break. Walls did not crack, windows did not shatter, the walks did not split. It was as if we were inside a snow globe and while we remained secured, our world turned upside down.

"What's going on?" Stella asked.

Like nothing had happened at all, the ground was motionless once more but for—

"The butcher's shop," Pip pointed to the building where our dinosaur had eaten its fill earlier. Except that the shop was no longer there.

"Where'd it go?" Stella asked. "A building can't just vanish, can it? Because I cannot imagine those insurance claims."

It was gone. In its place was an empty square field in the same rectangular lot as the shop. Several small saplings stood where a counter had once been. The elms soaked up the sun, as if they'd been there all along. "It didn't vanish," I realized. "It's as though the butcher's shop had never been built. The whole plot went back in time."

"The power is growing, Oliver," Nell said. "By my calculations and based on these fluctuations, time will stop at precisely twenty minutes of nine."

"8:40?" Stella asked. "AM or PM?"

It would be too generous for us to have until the next morning. That meant, "We only have a few hours."

Dodger asked the obvious question first. "What do you mean by time stopping? What happens?"

"Think of time like a long string," Nell said. "We start out from one end and continue, until our thread runs out. Or it's cut."

"Like the Fates of ancient Greece?" Pip asked.

"Precisely. We are all individual threads. But together, we're woven into a loom to form something more." I nodded at Nell's explanation, preparing myself for the twist that would knot up my understanding. So far, so good, but it was never that simple.

"But as we move closer to eight-forty tonight, more and more threads will be cut. The loom is becoming entangled," Nell continued, her voice rising from the watch like a scientist gone mad, "time won't stand still or stop. We won't be frozen in place like you might think. It doesn't work like that. Instead, that string will ball up. Every moment contracts into one."

And there it was. "I don't follow."

Pip, damn him, explained, "It means that everything that has ever happened or will happen can all happen at once. Right here, right now. Buildings disappearing, extinct creatures roaming the streets, far flung technologies unleashed in our present, it all entangles in a moment, in sort of a quantum state."

"Oh, that makes sense to me, too," Stella said. "Typical movie stuff."

"Quantum . . .?" I asked. How did Pip know this?

"If it's not Nell or Ollie's timepiece," Dodger pumped a fist, "Then who or what do we have to punch to stop it?"

"Whoever is doing this is breaking the natural law, the natural order of things. It's not governed by the Spirits. It's manmade," Nell said.

"That's never good," Stella said.

I could think of only one person who might uncover the knowledge and discover secrets of time-travel. He, above all else, would have a reason to bring the clock to a stop. But that was impossible for him to do. He was trapped in a hell I had made for him.

Or was he? Had he found a way to escape? Had he found a way to bring her back, the woman that he loved, that was stolen from him? I glanced at the time on my watch. Just to annoy me the minute hand clicked forward as I did. "We need a plan, quick. We don't have much time."

"Wrong again, son," a voice from past appeared from the shadows. It continued, "In a few hours, you will have all the time in the world."

A hunched-over figure stepped out onto the street to reveal himself. He had aged considerably. A long white mustache replaced burly brown and wrinkles had worn through sturdy cheeks that used to host a gracious smile. That was gone now. The man there was empty. Old. Almost no trace of the man I once knew existed in this skeletal visage.

Mr. Brownlow.

That man had once been like a father to me, as close as an orphan ever could have. The thought of facing him again made my stomach queasy and my heart ache.

"They say time is subject to no one," Brownlow said in a growling, raspy voice. "It abides me."

Part II

Chapter 14
Mr. Brownlow's Newspaper Part I

BROWNLOW'S PAST, YEARS AGO:
"What are you doing? You can't leave me here," Brownlow demanded. He could hear in his voice his own shock of disbelief and anger. The damnable ex-urchin *did* leave him here, stranded in time. Copper swirled in front of him on the grated catwalks high above his steam-works as Oliver and Edward vanished and Mr. Arthur Brownlow was alone. Oliver had called it a fate of his own design. But it was Oliver who had been too blind to see his plan. He had just wanted to make London better.

It was all Oliver Twist's fault! Oliver was an orphan who he had taken in and raised as his own. His own *son* had abandoned him. Twist had left him within the hellscape of a burning London that the boy had created, not him. Fire raged like a serpentine dragon flying over the city against the backdrop of a black-orange sky. Flames licked at him even here on his perch high above the ruin of his life's ambition. The catwalk dangled precipitously over the dark waters of the Thames . . .

If the boy had only listened, London would have become a far better place for all its law-abiding citizens. And proper Londoners would never lose someone they loved to the filthy parasites of the city again.

He had lost the woman of his dreams – and on their wedding day. A picture of brains and beauty, Helena was as lovely and delicate as a crystalline bouquet of orchids. Those were always her favorite flowers;

she especially liked those with pink-purple hues. Her hair held them as she took her turns strolling through London's various gardens, particularly those of Hyde Park.

It wasn't the walks themselves that Mr. Brownlow disapproved of, it was that she chose to walk alone, without him. Usually, he didn't mind. He had his books to attend. But at other times, while he was holed up safely in his fortress in Pentonville, he felt it was dangerous for her to go alone. After all, he'd recently been robbed of a handkerchief during his last excursion out to the city.

And look where that had landed him.

As always, Miss Leeford, soon-to-be Mrs. Brownlow, took her morning constitutional, along with a small change purse for people in need. She would strike up kind conversations with strangers whilst in the parks where she would learn each one of them by name. There was Mrs. Brown, the widow who'd been evicted from her home upon her husband's passing. The boys Harry and Thomas who were two too many mouths to feed and therefore had been abandoned by their parents. The Redcoat Footguard with one foot missing from war, who couldn't find employment because of it. To each, she slipped a ha'penny whenever she could. And she would recite her adventures to him each day, unknowingly interrupting his reading.

Until one dawn, the day of her wedding, a pair of thieves had learned of her small coin purse and of her daily habits. The mugging must have gone wrong. Brownlow didn't know what had happened for sure. No one had, for some peculiar reason. Only that a pistol had fired and with that single bullet ended the promise of the lovely lady Leeford.

Though details the Yard had provided him were scarce, they had retrieved her timepiece. With trembling hands, he opened it while standing in the doorway of his fortress. The crystal inside the silver watch had cracked. Time had stopped. Her world, and by virtue of their impending marriage, his world too, had ended at precisely eight-forty a.m.

***

The railing had grown hot. Too hot. Mr. Brownlow broke free of his reverie. He hadn't even realized that his hands had been gripping the steel railing. The heated metal had burned them like a frog in a pot slowly being brought to boil. The steel supports of the catwalk creaked under the strain of heat and weight. He knew that they would give way soon and he would plunge to his death.

He gazed into the damning waters of the Thames churning blackly below. Those waters had brought life to his steam-works. Its waters powered the engines from within his giant factory that stretched across the river. Perhaps they could offer him life as well, damned as he was. With a blind leap of faith off the catwalk, he fell past the licking flames and into the roiling blackness below.

***

Helena, he thought, as the waters took him. *Oliver Twist*. The name came out a curse. The time-traveler. Somehow, the boy had unlocked the secrets of time. But if a boy could manage, it was possible for him as well. He would discover for himself those secrets and use them to escape the Faustian prison Twist had locked him in. He would escape and enact revenge. But not just revenge. For if he possessed the secrets of time, he could bend it to his will . . .

***

He knew exactly what he would do.

He emerged from the waters with a renewed sense of purpose, baptized by London's waters and the fires of the very city itself.

***

What does one do with a time-machine? Travel to the ends of the earth to see what fate awaits? Use it as a tool for scientific discovery? Dive back to the time of the dinosaurs? Zoom ahead to witness the birth of deep space exploration? To prove or disprove faith? To learn how the Pyramids were built or rescue the lost manuscripts of Alexandria? So many possibilities. None of them were entertained, of course. Mr. Brownlow had but two purposes: to save his fiancée and enact revenge.

He needed to build the time-machine first. For that, he needed help from an old friend. Bertie drank too much and talked too heavily. From his drunken ramblings, Brownlow deduced that his mate had stumbled onto something, something huge. Rumors gave way to facts and facts gave way to an admission that Bertie had a prototype in progress. But what was he building?

On one occasion, Bertie showed him a newspaper. But it wasn't any old copy of *The Times*. This edition had a printed date of "1971" – over a century into the future. There was an article about an American Apollo mission, and something called a computer. A misprint? A hoax? Mr. Brownlow didn't think so.

Bertie was thickly mustached and broad-shouldered, possessing a pugilistic countenance which was entirely undercut by his nickname, which he preferred, over his given name of Herbert George Wells.

Bertie was considerably younger than Mr. Brownlow but also one of the few men more brilliant. Yes, Bertie had managed to bring from the future a copy of the *London Times* from 1971. But that wasn't enough. That had been only a small, simple trial. To fling Brownlow forward or backward through time, he would need something bigger. And Bertie would help him build it.

***

It was a marvelous wonder. The time-machine looked like a small stage about the size of a horse. On that stage was a velvet chair, fit for a throne. The front consisted of a control station, reminiscent of a truncated church's pulpit. The analogy was not lost on Brownlow, who would soon master both Faith and kings.

A rather large and ostentatious concave clock sat at the rear of the strange craft. The analog clock helped control where and *when* in space-time the craft could go by the precise movements of its hands, along with other gyros, timepieces, and computational devices that measured things such as the Earth's orbit and rotation.

Around the clock, extruding on either side, were copper pipes flanking the contraption like a ribcage, protecting its important organs: the steam-powered engine and difference-machines that further powered, controlled and computed coordinates for the time-machine.

Altogether, it looked like a one-person sleigh, one that Father Christmas would envy. It stood as a testament to the ingenuity of Man's triumph over gods themselves. More importantly, the time-machine had one last quality: after a decade of research and testing, it *worked*.

"We need more time." Bertie clutched the edge of the table. He must have realized that his tea had been drugged by now.

"That's the idea," Brownlow replied through a low chuckle.

"We don't know what could happen at such a scale. We could cut through the very threads of the universe." Bertie shook his head, a tear let loose down his cheek. It wouldn't kill him, only put him to sleep for a long while, but there was no way for Bertie to know that as he struggled to remain conscious.

Brownlow fanned his wool coat to cool himself. It had grown warm in the kitchen. Usually, he hired others for knife-work like this. He tapped his foot on the worn wooden floor of Bertie's kitchen, waiting for the laudanum to work.

"You could collapse cause and effect completely, stop linear time as we know it," Bertie pleaded. His head hit the table hard enough to rattle the rose-petal ceramic tea set that Brownlow had gifted his friend for his birthday earlier that year.

"Interesting observation, my dear friend," Mr. Brownlow said. "And thank you, thank you for everything."

Bertie slipped into sleep. Brownlow felt nothing except for his age. He looked down at skeletal hands. His fingers ached, his back burned, and he had grey thinning hair instead of robust brown. But the unkind years had borne fruit: Mr. Brownlow had his contraption.

He stole into the time-machine and input the coordinates he'd memorized since that moment at his doorway so long ago.

The machine hummed to life. A white glow emanated from the clock's face and engulfed Brownlow and the machine. With a turbulent start, his surroundings soon vanished into time.

First, he would save her, then the world.

Chapter 15
Mr. Brownlow's Newspaper Part II

It was 8:38 in the morning when Mr. Brownlow's time-machine settled in the morning fog. The machine let out a long, dissipating, howling rumble, like a freight train slowing. A waft of foulness arose from his surroundings. If he hadn't known any better, he would have guessed that he had landed in a rookery rather than a park. But the tramps and vagrants who took refuge here bathed the gardens in an underworldly musk.

The time-machine, as far as he could tell, had performed quite admirably on its maiden voyage. He'd made it through relatively unscathed as well, aside from a sour stomach that threatened to spill over. But he pressed the contents back, stilled his spinning head, and began to search for evidence that he was in the right place and time. Satisfied that the instrument panel was correct, he peered through the fog at the people who had stopped to stare.

The tenants of Hyde Park: the Redcoat with one foot, a couple of children, a few drunkards, all gaped and exclaimed at the mysterious man and his strange manner of arrival. He caught the attention of two rail-thin sailors. One had blonde hair but had only one eye of bright blue, the other socket was as dark as night. The other man was shorter, but older, more grizzled. They both carried the air of hardened men, pressed into service from the gaols, no doubt to serve at Her Majesty's leisure.

No matter, they were no threat to him. Brownlow tapped his new Colt Pocket pistol he carried within his frock coat and acquired specifically for this mission.

Miss Leeford hadn't yet turned the corner and appeared out of the grove of thick, tall elms that packed this pocket of the park. But she would any moment. And when she did, he would protect her, by any means necessary.

He worried that she might recognize him, but wrinkles and worn clothing belied his identity. He would save her, hop back into the machine, and disappear entirely. His younger self, now wed, would live the happy life he had been denied while he . . .

Well, it wouldn't matter what happened to him, he thought grimly. Besides, she would be safe.

"Hey," a gruff voice came from behind. Brownlow ignored it. There was no time to tarry. Probably a beggar wanting coin anyway. The voice came again, this time, much closer. He could almost feel foul breath on his neck. "Hey, dapper fella, where're you goin'?"

Fingers fell onto his shoulders. The grip tightened, slowing him down. Why couldn't they leave him alone? Very well. Brownlow spun around and put a face to the voice. The tall sailor stood before him. And he wasn't alone. The older, more grizzled Navy man stood beside him, muscle and brains between them.

"Just what is that infernal . . ." the man scratched his face and pointed to the strange contraption that had appeared out of nowhere.

"Machine?" The other answered.

"Yeah, that's right. I've been in ports in places you don't know exist, but I ain't never seen one of them." The gruff voice dipped lower.

"It's none of your concern."

"You must be loaded, cracked, or both with a machine like that." He slid out a rather pointy looking blade. To his mate he said, "Just his fine clothes could fetch a nice price. You want him to strip? We wouldn't even need to empty his pockets."

"Ah, now you've gone and gave the game away," the shorter man said, "What'av' I told you about that?" He slid out a long, thin knife as well.

"Oh, right. I thought he knew he was gettin' mugged."

Mr. Brownlow did not freeze. His only thought was, *these could be the men that had robbed and murdered Helena.* Or were they? She'd been shot. These men only had knives. Maybe one of them had a hidden gun. It was a bit confusing and happening so fast.

The clock on his time-machine audibly clicked to 8:39. These two dunderwhelps were going to ruin everything. He pulled out his pistol shakily to the surprise of the other two. But neither stepped back. Instead, they seemed to steel themselves. He jerked his pistol between the two of them as they started to circle him. He turned with them, as if in some sort of macabre dance. Pointing his shaky sidearm at the larger man, he said, "You, you're a murderer. You killed her. Drop your knife or I'll I drop you."

"Now wait a minute, I ain't killed nobody." The taller moved closer. Brownlow spotted a rash under the man's chin and small red stains on his shirt. Were those faded spatters of blood? "And neither have you. You're not goin' to start with me, mate, are you?"

"Feel free to test that assumption," Brownlow bluffed. But his voice cracked, betraying his intentions. At that, both men closed the gap and rushed him.

"Nick his coin purse, forget about the finery," the short man barked.

"No, I want it all, I'm hungry."

Brownlow was no longer facing his time-machine. He'd slowly spun around until he faced the wooded trail ahead. So, he could not see the clock click over to 8:40, and over the scuffle of violent footfalls, he did not hear it either.

The taller one swung his knife down. Brownlow fired. For an instant, all three stood frozen as the single shot echoed through the gardens. When nothing happened, the men redoubled their efforts.

"Get the gun!" The shorter one said. The two men were on him. He felt a strong grip on his hand, forcing the weapon lower. Brownlow writhed away but it was not enough. It was all he could do to avoid the sharp point of their blades, let alone keep a hold of his Colt. They pried it out of his hands. He dove forward, charging, anything he could do to get the gun back.

He picked it up again and raised it to a plethora of hands over his. It fired. He wasn't sure who had pulled the trigger. It could have been him. The men froze. Each looked down. The two sailors stepped back as Brownlow staggered. There was no pain. Not really. Just a punch in the gut. That was it. He couldn't have been shot. But an inspection of his midsection by his right-hand revealed blood. His toes felt cold, deathly. The pain hit: a stinging sensation, small at first, one that started in his gut but grew in length and intensity, radiating out to his back. A quick hand under his coat revealed blood there too.

He wanted to double over, to protect his wound, but to do that would be to surrender to the encroaching cold he felt creeping from his toes to his legs. He didn't want to die. He wouldn't.

The two men were still there, knives out, faces aghast. They looked up, but not at him, past him, as if he weren't there. He heard a moan from within the paths of the woods. It was followed by a weak but recognizable call for help. The one-legged soldier, who'd stood by watching, hobbled quickly to answer the call, as if he'd known the voice. Others followed.

"Bollocks," one of them said. "The bloody Peelers will be here any moment, grab his purse and let's go." Thus robbed, the sailors fled, flying past the time-machine and into the foggy abyss beyond his sight.

The low moan turned into a howl of pain.

Pain?

It hurt him to walk but he had to see the scene for himself. A few painful moments later, he saw it: a young lady in a flowery day dress was coughing up blood. She lay on the path while the others surrounded her. The soldier called for a surgeon, and another raced away for help. He knew her, didn't he? What had he come here for?

He approached the woman, her coughing growing louder, her breath more erratic, he lowered himself to her. He knew her.

Impossible.

"You," the soldier accused. "You shot her."

No, that couldn't be. His thoughts muddled. Had his first shot gone wild? Had he shot her?

No.

He propped her in his lap, her long golden hair fell across his legs as he supported her head, the fragrance of her orchid-scented perfume rising to meet him. "No, no, no," he sobbed.

"Arthur?" she raised a hand to his cheek and smiled at him. Her smile faded to concern. "You look different, sad."

"I am, dear, I am." Brownlow cried. "I've missed you so much."

"It's strange, this feeling. It's as if time is slowing down and the world has melted away. Don't be sad, Arthur," she said weakly. "We have all the time in the world."

He hugged her, even as her last wet breath rattled.

No. Brownlow ran bloody fingers through her hair. He shut her eyes and gingerly traced her cheek.

No. This wasn't happening, he would never do such a thing, he could never do such a thing, it hadn't been his fault, he had only tried to help, he could make this right – he had a bloody time-machine, he could fix it. He could make it right.

No.

Something she had said about time.

It was *time*, fate itself, laughing at him, belittling him, preventing him from doing what he thought was right. The universe itself was against him. First, it had sent the boy to stop his steam-works, then it had killed his fiancée.

The time-machine couldn't fix this. Bertie had warned him that this could happen, hadn't he? That scoundrel. Bertie had said that outside scientific inquiry, use of the time-machine could, "cut the very threads of the universe. Stop time." But Bertie hadn't warned him that something like *this* could happen. The fool.

Stop time. The words ticked through his head.

Her timepiece lay cracked beside her. She had carried it this morning so she could keep track of the time, she had told him a lifetime ago, otherwise she'd likely be late to her own wedding. He picked up the watch. He didn't need to look at the face to know what time it was.

Peelers' whistles shattered the still moment like the shattering of stained glass of Westminster Abbey.

"Goodbye, my dear," he said, placing her head on the cold ground. Bleeding, he picked himself up and staggered back to that infernal machine, picking up his only means of protection, his pistol, on the way. He had to get out of here, anywhere, anytime. It didn't have to be far. He hastily clicked a few dials a few short turns at random and gave one last longing look at the woman he loved and said to her, "I will see to it that I see you again."

He pressed the button that would start the machine as nebulous tendrils of a new plan began to coalesce. The time-machine vanished with a whoosh as Peelers piled onto the scene.

Chapter 16
Mr. Brownlow's Newspaper Part III

He slammed into a series of thin, white tree trunks, and bounced along muddy marshes before the time-machine came to a stop half-submerged in the mud. The difference machine sparked. Copper pipes had become entwined with tree branches, and Mr. Brownlow himself was thrown hard against the dials of his console, shattering several of them. New injuries on his arms and hands ran with fresh blood.

He arose with a groan. All things considered it was a small scientific miracle that he'd survived. Considering the motion of the universe, the rotation of the planet, the sheer mathematics of it all to have landed in one piece and not stuck out in space or inside a mountain made him say what amounted to a prayer to Saint Newton and Pythagoras the Pious.

The time-machine was damaged; he could tell by the whine of the engine and the sparks and pops from the difference-engine devices. He was stuck here (wherever 'here and when' were) until he could fix it. But the tools and material might not even exist yet. He might be here for some time. Most of all, aside from a few trinkets he might possibly pawn, he was broke. Of course, all the money in the world would be worthless right now if he had landed in a time before proper medical care.

Brownlow, in some significant measure of discomfort, went through the provisions Bertie had prepared. He tossed a case of clothing aside and a few broken jars of jerky and salted pork, before finding the first aid kit.

Rifling through the case, he moved past a near-empty vial of laudanum to find a hypodermic needle prefilled with morphine. Yes, it had been costly – hypodermic needles were not as common as necessity dictated, especially with the Civil War raging on in the States. But the costs and preparation had been worth it. Bertie, if anything, was always prepared. In this case, his over-caution had come in handy. As the pain medication kicked in, he bandaged both the entrance and exit wounds on his abdomen, thankful that the bullet hadn't lodged itself in him. He hoped no vital organs had been hit.

He left his ruined time-machine, searching the area for any hints that could tell him where he was. He thought he might have been in the moors. In the distance, he caught sight of a bleak house through a rolling curtain of grey mist.

It wouldn't do to walk up and say, "Please help me fix my time-machine." He might be run off with pitch forks, or worse, imprisoned. No, he'd have to be more cautious, more cunning.

He continued his search, passing by a forge (which would be vital in repairing his craft, he knew) and soon found himself in an old cemetery. There were muffled voices ahead, unusual in such a place. One of the voices sounded like it might belong to a large man, who spoke in threatening tones. Another voice answered. It was a boy. He stopped, crouching out of sight behind a stone marker.

It wouldn't do any good to interfere. He'd have to double back. He'd seen a couple of prison hulks floating heavily out in the waters some distance from the forge. He'd have to keep away from them too, as it would be inconvenient for him to run up against any British patrols.

Then again, he needed help. The bandage and morphine would only last but awhile, his time-machine had to be fixed. And he still didn't know where or when he was. He had to do something, didn't he?

He un-pocketed his pistol as his mind raced with choices. Something the sailor said to him earlier gave him pause. Mr. Brownlow was not a killer. He'd hired others to do that type of work, but he'd never pulled a trigger himself.

But if he had . . .

If he'd shot those two sailors without hesitation, Helena would still be alive, wouldn't she?

He listened awhile longer, as the boy struggled and yelled. He crept in for a closer look. Among the mossy headstones and low-lying brambles of the cemetery, he spied the boy's assailant.

The man was large, bald and angry. He was barefoot and his feet were bloody. He was covered in thick mud and tattered clothing. Chains around his legs and arms clacked and rattled as he roared, terrifying the upended child. The boy was of strong build, at the age of apprenticeship, struggling against the escaped prisoner. A fleeting thought raced through Brownlow's head: an apprentice.

Yes.

Brownlow quickly hammered out a plan, stood up, took aim . . .

And fired.

Chapter 17
Mr. Brownlow's Newspaper Part IV

LONDON, OLIVER TWIST'S PRESENT DAY:
Finally. Mr. Brownlow straightened his shoulders. After many, many treks through time to gather the allies and supplies he would need to finalize his plans, he was ready to light the stage and bring up the curtain. *Showtime.*

It had taken nearly a decade to make the repairs to his time-machine. It had taken days to dig it out of the muck and drag it via horses to an abandoned barn under the cover of night, with Pip's help. The difference-machine had needed parts that didn't exist. The frame and copper piping that provided power, and the steam-engine itself, needed delicate blacksmithing and mechanical know-how to repair.

For that, he had Pip. The boy had made an excellent blacksmithing apprentice to his uncle, and as he learned and perfected his craft, repairs were made. Slow and secret. Slow. And secret.

His funds remained dangerously low despite selling anything he could (except for the cracked timepiece that belonged to his fiancée). While the craft was under restoration, Mr. Brownlow had made connections with a London lawyer. Soon, Brownlow's fledgling funds and investments matured into a sizable pool of wealth. By then, the lawyer had grown suspicious of Brownlow's seemingly impossible clairvoyance.

So, Mr. Brownlow had sent Pip to the city "to be made into a gentleman." But really, he was there on Brownlow's behalf. Jackpot predictions of speculation were seen in a different light when it was a young upstart making the trades. Even so, it had taken some measure of time to rebuild his wealth, for investments, even surefire ones with the benefit of foreknowledge, took time to mature.

In the ensuing years, grey had completely overtaken him. He could no longer stand fully upright, and his gut wound had never properly healed from a horse surgeon's patchwork repair and stitches. Mr. Brownlow should have been miserable after everything that had happened. Instead, he smiled.

Almost ten years to the day that he had become stranded in the moors, his time-machine was complete. With a decade of planning behind him, Mr. Brownlow knew exactly every step that he must take. Years blinked back and forth at every trip Brownlow took to set his stage.

Now, his time-machine was smaller, sleeker, with Elm-Chip powered quantum computers instead of difference-engines, electric batteries powered by the sun instead of steam, and all the wealth and knowledge in the world he could want.

But Brownlow didn't want wealth and knowledge. He wanted his fiancée back. And if, somehow, he was denied that which his heart most desired, he would settle for killing the boy who had wronged him: Oliver Twist.

After stumbling a moment from age and the effects of time-travel, he stood as proud as his hunched back would allow and with pep in his step. This was the correct time. The correct place. It was time. He had come to conquer.

Each trip in his machine had, as Bertie warned, cut a different thread. That had been by design. This reality was already closing in on itself. If that didn't stop the boy and his friends, the army that Brownlow had brought along would.

Shadowy figures, each thick as trees and armed with axes, shields, and swords swarmed the street. Battle hardened warriors of old, each with red or blonde hair, skin paler than even a Briton's, were ready and willing to accept his orders, so long as the smashing of skulls was in order and the payment in mead and gold was provided.

With his time-machine, he could muster an army and resources so grand that he had only to stretch out his hand to the throne of Britain itself. But how long would a crown last? He had but a few years of life left. What meaning would a kingdom hold, or a world even, without his bride by his side?

No, he only had one choice, one chance. His plan, decades in the making.

His warriors stayed within the shadows of the dark alley awaiting his signal as he disappeared around a corner. Brownlow discovered that Oliver had allies too. Of course he did. But what Oliver did not know was that Brownlow held the ace. He knew Oliver's every move. He had seen it for himself.

"We don't have much time," the boy had said, unaware of Brownlow's arrival.

"Wrong again, son," Arthur Brownlow said. "In a few hours, you will have all the time in the world."

If he could not go to her, save her, he would instead bring Helena here, and stop the clock itself. There would be no more suffering. No more death. No entropy. Because there would be no more time. "They say time is subject to no one," Brownlow said. "But it abides me."

Part III

Chapter 18
Betrayal

"I'm assuming that's our villain?" Pip asked, knuckles up, stance wide as if the two would resort to fisticuffs. The chain of the timepiece dangled out from between tightened fingers. "Wait, he looks familiar."

I knew Brownlow well enough that he would never get his hands dirty, no matter how depraved his scheme. Of course, this Brownlow seemed different, colder, as if he had killed and would kill again. The man standing in front of us at the edge of the street within a couple of arm's lengths, was not the same. He was withered, worn, like leather left out in the sun. Grey and hunched. But his eyes burned like two pieces of fiery coal.

I pulled Pip back with me. This Brownlow, older and less physically threatening, was more dangerous than ever. Pip, Dodger, Stella, and I, along with our hopeful allies – the small band of Zulus – faced off against the single old man. We were outmatched, and Brownlow knew it.

"Mr. Brownlow?" Pip asked. His hands opened and his shoulders slouched. The watch in his hand was exposed. "I don't understand."

"You've gotten bigger, Pip, since last I saw you." Brownlow's eyes were on me, even though he was speaking to Pip, taunting me with the truth. "You'll get no grand speeches from me, young men. It's already too late, my plan has been in motion for some time."

As if on cue, the street shook. A small tremor, but an omen certainly of the things to come. We held our ground, but for a moment during the shaking, there was uncertainty in our stance. "I've finally outwitted you, Twist. You and your foundlings are finished."

"Where are the children, are they safe?" Stella asked after the shaking stopped. She looked pale, worried. There was panic laced into her question. "This whole city is about to erupt."

"I've got them at the Curiosity Shop," Dodger answered. I kept a sigh of relief to myself. Like Theseus' ship, the Curiosity Shop was the little place that kept surviving. It had originally been built from reclaimed wood from the London fire of 1666. It was over two hundred years old before Dodger herself had set the shop ablaze. But I had, at great expense, rebuilt it with its original bricks reformed from the ash. It was where I operated as The Orphan, where Nell had once tinkered, and where Dodger had built the steam-cycle. "Safest spot in the city."

"Good," Stella returned.

"Let's get to the point," I said to my adoptive father. "Tell us what you want." I thought I already knew. Nell had given us hints and told us enough, anyway. But if he could tell us more, overshare, say something that could help ensnare or stop him . . .

"You needn't know my intention. But I assure you, it's a showstopper."

"Some plan," I lied. "I know what you want. You want to unravel time, and you would use Pip against me." I watched Pip's eyes carefully, looking for the expected response, the stone-face that would have given away his sabotage. Instead, I saw . . . shock? Or was that hurt? Were there tears in his eyes?

"What are you on about?" he asked. "I confess to knowing Mr. Brownlow, he came to me as a child. I helped him and in return he made me the man I am today, but I've no loyalty to a villain. If I had known, I would have renounced him and spent my years with Uncle Joe on the moors."

"Yes, of course, of course," Brownlow jested, "Pip performed admirably, but I knew he could never betray you, you're too good. No, my expectations were greater and more twisted than putting my faith in a mere boy from the marsh. Pip was never my plan."

"I'm more than the moors," Pip said, with a reddening face, "You . . . you needed me."

"Indeed. But you served your purpose. I have no further use for you just as you had no further use of that place you called home. You left your Uncle Joe. Tell me, how long has it been since you've visited him? Played knaves with him? How ashamed of him were you when he brought the muck from the moors to your doorstep here in London?"

"How could you know about that?" Pip's face was still red, but not red from anger. I felt my own blood flush my cheeks in a similar fashion to his, for I'd been fooled too. I thought Pip had it all. Wealth, fine clothes, more money than he could ever spend. But in the end, what did Pip possess? What had he given away to get what he had?

"You're not in his pocket?" I still found it hard to believe. "But what about leading me away?" I should never have left Dodger and the foundlings. That certainly had to be by design, hadn't it?

"No, Oliver," Brownlow laughed. It was a hoarse, gravelly laugh, the kind that you would expect to hear haunting a cemetery at night. "That was *you* wanting what *he* had."

"I'm sorry, Oliver, I thought it was a grand idea, getting that gatling gun," Pip pleaded. "I was delighted when you agreed, taking in the big picture. You're not saying that it was a mistake, are you?"

Dodger cast me a look that could crack stone. Her disappointment in me, my false accusations of Pip. Brownlow was playing us perfectly. Incredible. There was not a single accusation that I could lay at Mr. Brownlow's feet. I'd done this to myself. Goosebumps swarmed my skin as I made another cold realization. "What about my watch?"

I'd given it to Pip freely and only afterwards did I realize my mistake. But, if Pip was truly my ally, it was still in safe hands. For now. I wouldn't feel that it was completely safe until I had it back, before it and Nell's essence ended up in the wrong hands. I held my hand out eagerly, expectantly, as if I was back to being a boy again with a bowl out asking for more. "Pip, I'm going to need you to return that."

"Oh, yes, of course, Oliver, I didn't mean to keep it so long, here—" Pip held out the watch.

"I'll take that, thank you," Stella stole the timepiece from Pip's outstretched and opened hand. He hadn't seen it coming. Neither had I. She strutted away from us over to Mr. Brownlow, flashing us all a crooked smile and looking very pleased with herself. She did some sort of momentary victory dance, as if for an audience that wasn't there. "Feels good to finally break character. I am *not* a method actor."

I could have kicked myself. I'd been thinking so poorly of Pip that I hadn't seen Stella stab my back. My soul shredded itself. She had my watch. And by all appearances she didn't look as if she'd be giving it back.

"And the Tony Award goes to . . ." Stella slow clapped, stopped and shook her head. "It's unfortunate that no one here knows what that means, what good is a performance if you don't earn an award? I guess *this* trophy will have to do." She took a bow and blew kisses while waving the watch around. "Thank you, thank you."

"Of course, the first girl I find fascinating turns out to be evil," Pip said.

"Don't feel bad, she fooled us all," I offered.

Dodger waved my words away. "Not me."

Pip ignored Dodger's quip and pleaded with Stella. "Why?"

"Do you know how much tuition is?" Stella answered stony-faced. "I don't need that kind of debt."

As bad as I felt about being taken in by Stella, I felt worse for Pip. I knew he liked her from the moment he pulled her out of the rubble. That's where Pip's mind was at too, "But what about . . ." he fumbled, "I mean, you and me?"

"I'm an aspiring actress, Pip, it's my job to play pretend."

Pip retreated inward, proud shoulders slinking down, eyes cast low, like a puppy that had been kicked by Brownlow and run over by Stella. In fact, his eyes were welling. He wiped away any evidence with a sleeve and tried to stand more stoically but by then, the game was up. "You really don't care for me?" Pip squeaked.

Stella sighed, her voice lowering. "Look, I appreciate you saving my life. Stupid me got stuck in that building, and you pulled me out. But I have my whole career ahead of me, Pip. Unless you can conjure an oatmilk latte and some friendly conversation, it's not going to work out between us."

There was silence between them as the truth sank in.

"Enough," Brownlow snapped. "We have the watch, and we'll have the foundlings. You can try and stop me or save them, that is, if you survive the coming moments. Either choice is futile in the end. You do not win."

"Ollie, let's stick 'im with a spear and be done with it," Dodger said. I'm surprised she hadn't taken out a pepperbox pistol and shot Brownlow by now. She must be getting soft.

"Don't kill him," I said. "We need him to talk. Tell us how to stop this."

"Stop?" Brownlow coughed. He looked as if the first one to stop him would be the Reaper, not us. But he regained his composure enough to taunt us. "Oh, Oliver. I have a time-machine. I've seen the future. No, Oliver, I've already won, you tried, you failed. I've seen it happen. I arrived *from* that future. I've only come here to see it all play out. You know how I've always loved a good story."

An explosion of black powder cracked the air. I stood corrected. Dodger had just waited a tick longer to fire. The barrel of her pepperbox was smoking. Brick shattered into a dust cloud where Brownlow had been standing. To my astonishment, he'd sidestepped the shot without so much as a blink. "Time-travel, remember?"

I remained there, motionless, without a clue how to defeat Brownlow. Dodger was out of tricks, and without my watch, I was out of time. I watched helplessly as Mr. Brownlow took out a curved animal bone, maybe from an ox, and gave it a raspy, rattled blow. The sound, deep and rich, filled the air, despite the weak breath.

"A war horn?" Stella asked Brownlow. "You got Boromir back there?"

"Something like that," he answered. "You have your mission, they have theirs, meet at the rendezvous point when you're done."

Before Stella could leave, a horde of burly men and women warriors crashed through the streets with a rumbling war cry. About two dozen, from what I could see, began to surround us. They had low, fierce brows, even the women. Some had dark eyes and dark hair, others were blond or red. Each wore armor of animal skins dyed in colored patterns that I did not recognize. Some carried axes, others sharp swords. They all looked like they'd dealt death before.

"Vikings," Stella said, her eyes wide. "Fun fact: They don't wear pointy hats and paint their faces. But they are brutal." As she spoke Brownlow disappeared within the forming horde.

"What a waste of a time-machine," Pip said. "The things we could learn. I've always wanted to see the future, see what we're capable of."

"We're not likely to live long enough to see tomorrow," Dodger said in her usual comforting way.

The Zulus had earlier gathered as many spears, both the throwing and close-combat ones, as they could. But with what they had (assuming they fought with us) and Dodger's assorted menagerie of weaponry, my cane, and of course Pip's wit, we were outmatched and outnumbered.

I begged Mandla, "We need your help, we can't win without you."

He stood unspeaking, his spear held stiff like a staff. Had our truce broken? Had they been swayed by Stella's switch? Or would they simply abandon the battlefield and leave us to our fates?

If they did, Pip, Dodger, and I were dead.

Chapter 19
Battle

Mandla still didn't answer even as the horde swarmed ever closer from across the street. The sky exploded in color as the sun started its descent below the horizon. The evening fog would roll in soon. As the Vikings closed in, they unleashed a series of war whoops that would likely haunt my nightmares, if I would be so lucky to ever sleep again.

The Vikings were about to strike but there were still no assurances we had allies for the imminent battle ahead.

"We have considered your words and the words of your enemy," he said finally. He had not consulted with Solomon. He didn't need to. I could tell by their eager expressions. "We side with you. Finally, an adversary we can sink our spears into."

Energy soared as the Chief called his people, and they broke into a choral cry unlike those I'd heard before. This one seemed to sing to victory for even if they fell in battle, the translator explained, they would be welcomed by the open arms of their ancestors. From what little I knew of the Vikings, they felt the same way.

This would have been awe-inspiring if Pip, Dodger, and I weren't about to be cut to pieces. Pip pumped his fists and Dodger, who would undoubtedly duck her way out of combat somehow—

No, nevermind. She leapt first into the fray with a yell that surprised me. I don't think she had even reloaded her pepperbox before hurtling the otherwise worthless weapon into a woman warrior with dark eyes who was at me.

Dodger dove feet first into the Viking, kicking her down to the ground and making her lose her grip on her axe. It went flying. She landed hard while Dodger stuck her own landing as if posing for a Renaissance master. The Viking's axe bounced against the cobblestones and shot back at her. She rolled out of the way in time for Dodger to catch it mid-air. She slammed the weapon's broadside down on the downed warrior's forehead, sending her to slumber.

I had to admit it, I was impressed, not that I would tell her. Not that I had much time to consider before I had my own Viking to fight. He wasn't as small as Dodger's had been. The big, broad-shouldered Viking, wrapped in black fur, gripped a sword as large as I was. And he was coming right toward me. Why did I get the big ones?

I twisted out of the way as the sword came down. It must have been heavy, but he made it seem like a twig as his strikes came swift and hard. Even with my cane to help block the blows, I wouldn't be able to dodge or deflect them all. Another wide swing blew by.

Acting fast, I aimed the ball of my cane at the Viking. He wore an unadorned helm to protect his head. It narrowed my opportunity to land a clean strike, but I took the shot. The heavy brass ball burst out from my cane, striking true. *Take that.*

The Viking stood there, grinning. Blood ran down a broken nose, but he hadn't flinched. That shot had been my best chance to best him. Instead, he swung his sword down. I blocked it by holding my cane above my head with two hands, like it was an overhanging bar. He sliced through it like I'd been holding a carrot, my cane splitting into two pieces. But before the sword could cut into my scalp, it became entangled by the wire cord. I took the wire and wrapped it around his weapon. He considered it for a moment as if it were a fly that had been caught in a web before tossing the sword aside. As it clattered to the ground, he charged.

I readied myself, remembering what Nell had taught me about boxing. I'd faced a larger opponent before, and I knew it was possible to win this fight with the tools she had taught me, but I hadn't won that last fight without a few bruises and broken ribs of my own.

Crouching low and wide, as he came in overheard, I let fly a punch into the man's already broken nose. He'd taken the previous hit without a thought, but a second one, on a wound, sent him recoiling with a howl. I took the initiative to swing out my leg, something I'd seen Dodger do. My foot caught him as he moved backwards. He stumbled and fell, his helmeted head hitting the stones with a dull clang that sent him lights out.

Pip was punching his way out of a corner, until Dodger tossed him a sword she had taken from her current opponent. He caught it and brought it to block a blow that would have split his head. His stance shifted, one arm akimbo, the other holding the sword straight ahead. "It's not a gentleman's weapon, too thick and heavy," he said, swinging it around as if getting a feel for it, "but it'll do in a pinch."

The two Vikings, a woman with red hair, the other a bald man with a massive blonde beard, continued their assault, but Pip parried their attacks. He disarmed the redhead and slit her palm, putting her out of the fight for a moment. The other, Pip stabbed straight through. There was a squelching sound and a desperate wet breath, before the man fell to the street as Pip withdrew his weapon.

I hadn't wanted anyone killed, but as the battle raged around us, Zulus and Vikings clanged spears with swords, I realized it was an impossibility. It was us versus them, and the other side were playing for keeps. But there was a way out of this, I knew, if I could perhaps retrieve my watch.

Now where had Stella stolen off to? She held the key. Before I could find her in this melee, another Viking lunged at me, this one larger than the first.

With no time to prepare, and as unarmed as I was, I knew that the Viking's blow would be my last. His sword came down for the kill when a spear tore through him. He dropped the sword, clutching bloody fingers to the wound at his chest, and fell back in shock. I helped him to the ground with a blow of my own.

Breathing heavy thanks, I looked to see who had saved me. It wasn't just any Zulu warrior, it had been Solomon. His long, white beard was spattered with red. I nodded in thanks and at the honor. I'm probably the only British person so far that a Zulu Chief had ever spared.

The Zulus had taken the brunt of the attack by opening their ranks and opting for hand-to-hand combat instead of keeping a safer defensive formation. Dodger, Pip, and I would not be alive without them. But they were risking their lives for us.

Unless I could get my watch back, each wound or possible death would stick. I reluctantly left the others to focus on the Vikings as I threaded through the fight to find and confront Stella. I had to get my watch back. It was the only way to save everyone and defeat Brownlow.

I found Stella only an alleyway away from the fighting. She was hunched over that white rectangular object that glowed on one side. Could it be some sort of futuristic pocket-watch? She kept switching her sight between the object and the streets around her before she noticed my presence looming from behind. "I downloaded some Victorian maps before I left," she said to me without looking. "None of these streets are lining up."

"Welcome to London."

"I suppose you wouldn't happen to know the way to the Curiosity Shop, would you?"

"I mean, I do," I said, approaching her. "But I think I'll keep that to myself, if you don't mind." She turned. Gone was the stoic Stella from before. She didn't stand as tall, and her hands trembled. I pressed my luck and asked, "How does an aspiring actress go from stage to stooge?"

"It's not like that," she said in a soft voice, "But I think if you understood, you'd agree with him."

"You think I'd agree to him putting the foundlings at risk?" That was a hell of a thing to say, considering my actions earlier. Hopefully, she wouldn't pick up on that.

"He told me of your penchant for getting the children mixed up in your fights. You're always bringing them along. They're probably safer with me anyway."

Well, that stung. "In my defense, I tell them to stay put, but they never listen."

"Listen, Oliver, Brownlow's not just my employer." She put her hands on my shoulders. I couldn't tell if this was her attempt at winning me to her side or if she was being genuine. "I believe he'll do what he says, and I don't know that I disagree with him."

"He's dangerous."

She laughed as her brown eyes bore into mine, like pistons. "There have been enough deranged white men running around threatening to destroy the world. Eventually, one of them is going to do it. I believe Brownlow is trying to save it."

"Maybe," I said with a hint of a break in my voice. I was hoping she didn't catch that. However, there was another angle to this. I wasn't entirely sure what his plan was. Maybe he *was* trying to do good, but I knew the man he had turned into, and that man could not be trusted. If I kept this up, perhaps Stella would stumble and spill what he was up to, and more importantly, how to stop him.

Stella put her arms down but took another step toward me. I understood why Pip was so smitten, she was attractive and sharp, and even I was feeling weak against her seduction. "I don't understand why you and Mr. Brownlow broke apart. He wants what you want. He told me that's why you became The Orphan. To stop pain and sorrow. To keep others from experiencing what you've been through. I think you're a good man, Oliver, you want this as much as he does. You want to put an end to death."

So, it was more than just stopping time. Stella was right, I wanted this. I was so tired of losing loved ones. In fact, I was almost running out of loved ones to lose. And all the problems that this city had faced since I became The Orphan wore on me. I couldn't muster a response to Stella, I could only wonder who she might have lost to have felt the same way; that terrible sick feeling that twists you on the inside and crushes you, every waking day. And sometimes makes you do unfathomable things.

"Face it, you've lost this one, Oliver. You might want to start admitting that you're on the wrong side."

I thought about what she said, and I thought about my companions. The Zulus were fighting bravely but armed with short spears and animal skin shields against the steel and animalistic rage of the Viking berserkers, it was only a matter of time before our allies were defeated. Pip and Dodger's lives were on the line. Eventually, they would fall. All the while, the foundlings were in danger, and the clock's hands crept closer to Brownlow's favor.

We were beaten.

I don't know how Brownlow got his hooks into Stella, but whether it was by enticement or something tragic from her past that they had connected or bonded over, she'd sided with him and had done her job well. She was the only thing standing in my way. Once I had my watch, I could fix all this.

"I'm sorry, Stella. I've only ever been alone. I've never had a side but my own and the foundlings and I don't intend to start now."

Brownlow had told her about me. But he may not have told her that I had begun my childhood in the city as a pickpocket, a rather good one at that. And Stella was standing oh so close to me.

Almost had it . . .

Something screamed in the distance, a high-piercing animalistic cry, like that of a crow, but bigger. Much bigger. How big, I didn't know, but I was sure I didn't want to find out. Stella stepped away, taking with her my chance at pilfering her pockets. It hadn't been in the left one, but before I'd checked the other one, the cry came, and it was too late.

The sun had set. Gritty plumes of coal smoke from the factories would soon mix with the fog, and blanket London in a murky darkness. It made the sky hard to see, but both Stella and I sent our eyes skyward, squinting into the haze.

There were many of them, a swarm, or perhaps a flock. Like bats with long, leathery wings and narrow, sharp beaks. I didn't think anything that big could fly. As they dove closer, I could make out feather quills on their heads. They weren't birds, nor bats, but they were big and strong enough to scoop us right up either in their eagle-like talons, or to gulp us down like fish trapped in a bucket.

I hoped that they would fly right past us.

But hope was running short on time today.

Chapter 20
Terror From Above

"Dreki!" a Viking yelled from down the alley. I left Stella to tear back towards the melee and the flock of sky-monsters that threatened my friends. As I breached once more into the bloodbath, I caught sight of the Viking leader. I slunk past him, thankful that his eyes were skycast so that I could regroup with the others in one piece.

To my surprise, Stella had followed me. Safety in numbers? Lost completely? Did she have something else to say? With one eye on the sky and the other on the Vikings, I knew that I also had to keep a wary eye on her too. I was running short on eyeballs.

The Viking chieftain was impressively sized, with a pelt of brown bear fur worn like a cape, no helm, and a thick plume of blond hair tied back. His war axe was equally impressive with a leather-wrapped handle and forged runic symbols inlaid into the double-bladed head. He looked as if he'd seen and survived a thousand battles. But as the beasts swooped closer, even he seemed shaken by the shadows in the sky.

He had called for the Vikings to halt their assault as he measured the possible new threat. One thin Viking held out a Zulu stabbing spear. My blood boiled at the thought of a Viking with such a blade, knowing how he must have won the weapon. The thin Viking said something that seemed to suggest, "I'll slay it."

"*Fifl*," the Chief said, his face reddening. There was something unmistakable, perhaps universally recognizable in curses. But the thin Viking didn't get the hint until it was too late. With a clumsy motion, he launched the spear (that was not meant for throwing) skyward. In a surprise to everyone, the blade hit true, piercing the body of the beast with a sickening sucking sound. The flying creature plummeted like a stone, landing on the cobblestones and sliding into a slow stop right before us all.

"That's not a dragon," Stella said in the confused stillness. "First, a Megalosaurus, now, a Pteranodon. My roommate is never going to believe me."

What a curious creature. The Pteranodon, or whatever she had called it, was dead. Its head was covered in blue and red feathers, but its wings were leathery, thin, and taut, like canvas over a kite's wooden frame. If the wings had been unfolded, they could have stretched from one side of the road to the other. Its long, narrow head was as big and sharp as a sword. I thought I'd stick with the Megalosaurus, thank you.

Meanwhile, the Viking chief had had enough of his insubordinate soldier. With a swipe of his regal war-axe, he separated the man's foolish brains from the rest of him. The head bounced down the street. Another new nightmare unlocked. I didn't approve of his punishment, but I wasn't about to argue either, for his blade was larger than my head and the beasts were upon us.

The Pteranodons swooped down, the street erupting into a cacophony of high-pitched calls and the flapping of leather. A small, downy covered Pteranodon plucked up the man's still bouncing head. It squelched like a grape inside the reptile's beak before it disappeared in one gulp.

"Get down and stay down," I called to everyone. We dove flat, bellies pressing against the cold, wet ground with the windy beating of the Pteranodon's wings above. It was like being caught in a windstorm.

"While I appreciate classification of those dinosaurs, Stella, I hope the next one makes a run for you, and carries you off," Pip said in a raised voice. Both he and Stella were prone, on either side of the street, facing each other.

"I deserve that," she replied. "But technically, they're flying reptiles, not dinosaurs. So my roommate says."

"You're so precise, Stella, if you weren't evil, I'd have bought you that coffee," Pip said.

"I'll drink it if you buy it," Stella said. "You'll thank me when this is over." She glanced at her glowing device and rolled over, facing the opposite direction. So that was why she had returned with me. Wrong direction.

"That way?" she asked herself out loud. After a moment that suggested she was weighing her choices, she spun across the street, deftly avoiding the fray with an acrobatic finesse that rivaled Dodger's.

"You wanna toss me back my watch?" I asked as one of the sharp-billed bird things stood in my way, blocking any hope I had at reaching Stella in time. She sped away, disappearing into the fog of chaos but going the wrong way again. The Curiosity Shop was down at the other end of the road. "I'll trade it to you for directions," I yelled.

My ploy went ignored as the Pteranodons swept through the street. Most of the Vikings dispersed as quickly as they'd attacked, flooding into alleys and indoors and anywhere a Pteranodon wasn't, but others still fought it out with the remaining Zulu warriors.

Pip and I played still, like possums, presuming that the flailing warriors made for more tempting targets. I'd lost track of Dodger.

From my low vantage point, I saw the Zulus, who had regrouped to form close-knit ranks. I couldn't help but notice sadly that their formation had shrunk. I thought they were being daft by painting a bullseye on themselves, but they stood their ground. As each Pteranodon swooped down, they sidestepped it, crouching in unison, letting it pass empty-clawed through their formation as they stabbed upwards in the air. The result was that after the first few Pteranodons attacked them, no further attempt was made. Impressive. Give these Zulus gatling guns and steam-engines and they'd conquer the world.

The Vikings had thinned as the thickest of the storm swept past. Stella reappeared, hunched over and crawling, heading in the opposite direction, on the correct route this time. Several Vikings followed her, each low to the ground and wary of the skies above. She said to me, sheepishly, "This way. I miss GPS."

I tried to roll across the street toward her, but a second Pteranodon sped past, flying just above my head. I don't know if it thought to make me a meal but a claw caught my shoulder. My skin opened into a blaze of white-hot pain as the claw tore through. I retreated, holding back a muffled yell.

I could do nothing but ball up and wait for the Pteranodons to pass. Blood soaked through my shirt and into my frock coat. Pressing my palm against the wound, I slowed the flow of blood, as Nell had taught me.

Soon, the clashing of weapons stopped, the Vikings retreated, and the sky was empty, replaced by night and a thick roil of pollution, chimney smoke, and fog. The bleeding had slowed to a trickle and my shoulder had numbed into a swollen red mess. That was going to leave a scar — another one for the collection.

"Wow, the Zulus didn't even flinch," Pip noted with awe in his voice. "Glad they're on our side."

The Vikings, I noted, as skilled and fierce as they were, had all fended for themselves. I winced as Pip bandaged my wound with an abandoned banner. It was white with a raven in outline on it, except now it was red with my blood. Pip pulled it tight, eliciting from my mouth a not-so-nice word.

"What about our friends?"

"I doubt the Vikings will return," I said. "They're likely falling back to wherever Brownlow was. Now we need to know the 'where' and the 'why' and the 'how' as in 'how to stop him'."

"Not why, I don't care 'why'. I want to stop Stella and end him, no matter their reasons."

I understood Pip and I was about to offer my sympathies when we noticed that the Zulus were motioning to each other. They were using rushed, anguished words and beckoning the wounded and the stragglers from the battle over to a prone figure.

Pip and I followed them. The Zulu leader was clinging to life. Blood gushed from a gash in his chest that ran from his neck down to his sternum, as if someone had tried to split him open along a long ragged line. It could have been from a Viking's blade or a Pteranodon's claw. My own shoulder ached in sympathy.

Pip and I drew closer, kneeling as we reached him. Everyone was silent but for the gurgle of what would likely be final words. After Solomon finished speaking, everyone nodded, as if in agreement. There was silence.

"What did he say?" I couldn't help asking Mandla. He did not answer me right away. Instead, he repeated back the words Solomon had said. Again, each member of the tribe nodded.

Finally, he answered: "It is an ancient Ubuntu proverb that unites all our people. *'I am because we are'*. With those words he lives on in our hearts, and our people, and in our people's future. So long as we exist, he will too."

I mulled these words over as I watched the life slip out of the once-proud Zulu leader.

Mandla closed Solomon's eyes. For a moment, all was still. But Mandla moved his eyes toward the street. He must have taken note of an object on the ground, glinting in the fleeting moonlight. He moved toward it, and I saw it for what it was: The fancy leather handle, the runic designs painstakingly crafted into the metal of the blade, there was no mistaking its owner and therefore, Chief Solomon's killer.

Mandla picked up the Viking's axe, cried out, and smashed the weapon blade first down on the rough, rocky road. The handle splintered into a thousand directions as the axe blade flew into the air before sparking as it landed and slid across the street.

Mandla howled and the Zulus began to chant.

Chapter 21
The End of a Friend

Pip and I stood there, reverently, heads bowed as the warriors mourned. But as time pressed on, I grew concerned. I was torn between grieving and our mission. I felt the best way to ensure that Chief Solomon's death was not in vain was to stop Brownlow, but I didn't know how to do that tactfully. I hoped sincerity would make the best approach.

I also did not know where Dodger had disappeared too. I assumed she was all right, but it's shaky to trust in assumptions. The last I'd seen her she was in the thick of fighting. The Pteranodons had swooped in, and I'd lost track of her. In the aftermath we'd found many slain bodies on the street and noted that others were missing. I hoped Dodger hadn't been taken by the Pteranodons or worse – killed.

"I must find my friend," I whispered as quietly as I could and hoped I could still be heard. "Pip and I must take our leave."

Mandla nodded approval, rose from a kneeling position he'd taken, and beckoned us to follow him. Away from the other mourners he told us, "We must return him to our lands so that he can receive the proper rituals for burial before our mourning and celebration can begin." He rubbed his hands together as if washing them, but Pip told me later that it was a ritual practice of purification. "He should not be left on this strange, foreign street."

"I don't know how to return you home, not yet," I said. I didn't want to give him false hope. The building next to the butcher's shop (or where the shop had been) was an apothecary with a long wooden counter. I pointed it out, saying, "Take Solomon inside there for now. Use whatever supplies you need for your wounded. We'll work to figure the rest out. I don't blame you if you decide to part ways from us until then."

"I'm sorry for your loss," Pip said. "You've saved many lives at the cost of your own, indeed, you've humbled me. I don't know what to say."

"Then say nothing," he said. "And do nothing to stop us. We will see that Viking dead." I didn't argue as Mandla curtly left us to carry their wounded and slain from the street. I still didn't know if Dodger was among them or if she had been saved by the Zulus as well. There was nothing to do but push through. Until I saw her, hatless, rising from the street.

There was some good news after all. I tamped down my enthusiasm, mostly because I didn't want her to see that I'd been worried about her. She'd never let me live it down. Still, she looked like she might have been injured.

She was holding her head and stumbling a bit. I didn't see any blood or wound. Wordlessly, she joined us and when she did, I figured out what had happened.

"You got knocked out, didn't you?"

"Never," she lied, but I wanted her to keep her dignity intact. It was as important to her as a magician's secret. Some illusions were worth believing in.

"Now that we're all here, except Stella—"

"Except Stella," Pip said sadly.

"We can concoct a plan, the three of us." Dodger finished.

"What about the foundlings?" Pip said. "They're in danger, and you told Stella where they are."

"No, I didn't." Another lie? I didn't think it was. It was one thing to fib over a matter of pride, like being knocked out in a fight, and another to deny what she'd said earlier to Stella.

Speaking of Stella, I decided to play peacemaker. "I don't think Stella will harm them." I believed it. She might not be on our side, but I didn't think she was fully on Brownlow's side either. "But this whole city is dangerous right now. It might be better if they were with us, to keep an eye on them." Yes, I know, the irony wasn't lost on me either. "We need to reach them before the others do. So, let's make haste to the Curiosity Shop."

"No, we don't need to go anywhere," Dodger mumbled.

Maybe she'd been hit in the head harder than I thought.

"You can come out now!" Dodger hollered.

The Zulus were filing into the red-bricked apothecary shop with their casualties. However, during a break in the stream, when nobody was walking in, three children stepped out.

It was the foundlings.

I stood there, in shock.

"How did you know to throw Stella off their scent?"

"I don't trust anybody. It comes in handy. Besides," she continued, after a swig from her flask that she placed on her forehead afterword, "I'm the Artful Dodger, I dodge trouble, artfully. It's in the name."

Clearly, she hadn't dodged everything thrown at her, but she'd come out alive, and she'd kept the foundlings safe. Their cuts, scrapes and bruises were all my fault. My blood began to boil, and my ego began to bruise. I wasn't proud of it, but I could tell that I wasn't completely in control of my emotions anymore. All I could do was watch myself grow angrier as I hugged each of my foundlings and took note of their wounds.

Edward, the oldest, held a bandaged arm tenderly. I recalled that Dodger earlier said that he'd almost lost it. I didn't know the details, but I could imagine them, and my guesses were grizzly.

Byron looked well except for a few scratches. He didn't need any more to deal with after the death of his brother Bertram. That pain was still fresh. All I could do was squeeze him tighter.

When Abbey came out, I was relieved that she was also uninjured but for some bruises. She'd grown so much and had lost much in the time I had known her. She'd become like family to me. All of them had. I knelt to face her at eye level and began to cry. She cried too.

And I felt each one of their cuts, abrasions, and bruises, as if they had happened to me. I glared at Pip through teary eyes. I'd almost lost everything because of him.

No, it wasn't his fault. It was mine. My choice. I knew that.

I didn't care.

The children were wounded, Dodger had realized she wasn't invincible, Stella had betrayed us, Pip had delayed us, my cane was destroyed, my watch stolen . . .

. . . and the Zulu leader was dead.

"We still have a chance," I said, shaking that feeling of failure off. I hoped it would stay off. But the thing about feeling like failure is that it never quite goes away. Dodger looked at me strangely.

"You didn't just throw Stella off the track, you sent her to the wrong train station. That buys us time and gives us a choice on how to proceed: We can go after her on our own terms, retrieve the watch, and ask Nell how to stop all this, or we can go after Brownlow blindly but take him by surprise. He'll assume we chose the children and won't suspect us."

"We don't even know where Brownlow is." This came from Pip. The question grated on me no matter how right he was.

"We have under two hours left, that's not time enough to go after both, we have to choose."

"Where would Brownlow be?" Pip asked.

"Why don't you know?" I snapped. "Weren't you deep enough in his pockets? Is this all an act like Stella's?"

"Pip doesn't know anything about it, do you?" Dodger asked while serving *me* the side-eye.

Ignoring them both and feeling more annoyed because Dodger had taken his side over mine, I reminded them, "Nell hinted he'd built his own time-machine. I don't think he built it into a pocket-watch or if that's even possible. I'm thinking it's big, so he needs somewhere large enough to house it, someplace to match the scale of his grand plan." I shook my head. "I don't even know where to start, what it might look like."

"Um, this is probably a bad time to say this, but I've seen it." Pip ran fingers through his hair.

"You've what?" Dodger's mouth went agape.

I grabbed him by his starched collars and pulled Pip closer to me. "Why didn't you say anything?"

"A time-machine?" he argued, "I was skeptical. It didn't work and I didn't think it ever did. I was wrong."

"I wanted to trust you." I was about to push him down into the street when Dodger grabbed my wrists.

"Let him go, let him talk."

After straightening his garments, he explained: "It's like a large sled in a way, about the size of a carriage without the horses." He lowered his head and placed a hand over his eyes "It's packed tightly with all sorts of machinery, it would need probably a lot of power to run, I think."

"Do you know where it is?"

Pip shook his head.

I was about to pummel him when Dodger said, "It could be anywhere, anytime." Since when did she start being sensible and stop wanting to bust in heads?

"Okay, so it needs power." I said, trying to calm myself down. Puzzles helped me think, and thinking relaxed me.

This time, it did not.

"He likely has a way to contain short amounts of power for the time-travel trips themselves, but he'd likely need to somehow recharge it." Pip said helpfully. "And for his scheme, whatever he's plotting, he likely needs more power. Much more."

"Steam?" Dodger offered. "Have we checked his Steam-works?" It was a good idea, but I'd already ruled it out.

"I don't think he'd return to a place where he'd lost before. And besides, Edward and I have kept that place under surveillance. He's not there." Edward nodded his head in agreement.

"There was a display on faraday discs—"

"We need to take a step back," I said, "look at what we're missing. This has got to be more than just stopping time, it's got to be personal. There's got to be a reason for it, a *why*. What do we know?" I cut Pip off, I didn't need to hear him speak right now. I wanted to *do* something. I felt like we'd been on these cobblestones for hours, stuck in some sort of three-person prison. My shoes were cutting ruts into the road.

"Time has been fracturing all day. Things from the past and future are all coming together here at this moment," she said.

"Maybe he's trying to bring something back?" Edward asked.

"Brownlow is searching for something, something lost in time, something he hopes to bring back here so that when time stops—"

I snapped, "It's not something, it's someone. I know where Brownlow is."

I'd laid orchids there this morning.

"Where would Brownlow have a grand place big enough and with enough power to power his machine?" Dodger asked.

"Where did the dinosaur first appear?" Edward asked again as if he were seated at the adult table. I suppose he was.

"Did I mention the lightbulbs and faraday generators?" Pip added.

"It is grand," Dodger said.

"And it has power." Pip offered.

We all nodded our heads and said in unison, "The Crystal Palace."

"We were already there!" I snapped at Pip. Our excitement was short lived for I was livid – the damned fool had led me astray. "If we'd never left, this would have been over by now. None of this would have happened."

"Oliver, this isn't Pip's fault."

I'd seen the state of the foundlings. I felt the slick stickiness from the blood of the Zulu leader on my hands. My stomach pitted that I'd lost Nell, the watch, and any plan to put an end to this. Perhaps Brownlow was right, I wasn't the one to stop him. Not this time. Suddenly, I didn't care that it wasn't Pip's fault, or anyone's, but I bloody sure was going to blame him.

"You helped him," I burst out like a dam giving way. "You took his gold, you fixed his machine, you, you lured me away. You're an accomplice even if you don't think you are. You're as guilty as Brownlow is." I knew this wasn't true, but I couldn't help myself from saying it. Nor could I help but punch Pip.

So, I did. I hit him. Right in the eye.

My fist collided with his face with a dull thud. He flew back from the surprise assault, landing on the ground. The foundlings gave out a whoop. Anything I did they saw through a filtered lens as if I were a hero. If they only knew the truth.

"Oliver Twist," Dodger said. "What's wrong with you?" She helped Pip up. "I don't know what's going on here but if anyone was going to punch you, Pip, I would have gambled that it was going to be me. Don't listen to him, he's wrong."

"No, he's correct," Pip confessed. "It's true that I helped Mr. Brownlow a long time ago. As a blacksmith's apprentice, I helped him fix his time-machine. In turn, he gave me gold enough to go my own way, to become a gentleman in London."

"You're not. You're nothing but a crook's accomplice."

"If I had known he was a criminal, I never would have helped him."

"You had a choice. The same one I had. Only I chose to turn my back on Brownlow. He was a father to me."

"And I turned my back on my Uncle Joe!" Pip yelled. "He was kind and made me laugh and protected me from my sister who used to hurt me. I left him to chase desire on a dime that wasn't mine. Don't you think I regret it?"

"You can be sorry all you want, but your part in all this is over. Dodger and I will take care of it from here."

"We need all the help we can get," Dodger said. "You're making a mistake. Don't you see that Pip was being lied to? That he was being manipulated from a young age like you were?"

"You made the best choice you had," she said to Pip. But to me she said something wholly strange, "People can change, you know."

That was not the Dodger I once knew, proving her point. Oddly, she had become a voice of sense. Perhaps this time it really was the apocalypse. But I was too stormy to hear her words and take them to heart.

"You're making a mistake," she warned.

"No, I'm fixing one."

"I've made my choice," Pip said, rubbing his eye. "You're right. I'm a risk. At the least, you can't trust me. I have affairs to settle, friends to see before the end, if it's to be." Pip began to leave. "Tally-ho, good luck, and all that, chaps."

He walked away and out of our lives. Hopefully, for good.

"Oliver! You make it hard for me to . . ." her voice trailed off.

"What?"

"Nevermind. It's you and me and the foundlings now. We're burning through friends faster than coals at Christmas. What are we going to do?"

I looked at a nearby steam-clock since I no longer had the timepiece. Our argument had cost us precious minutes. "We don't need Nell to stop Brownlow's time-machine. If it was broken once we can break it again. If Stella returns and tries to stop us, we'll stop her." I was feeling a little calmer since venting and Pip's subsequent departure, though my knuckles still hurt. Pip had a thick head.

"I think you're over-ambitious," she said. "Stella has the watch and an army. Brownlow certainly has other surprises in store. He's not going to leave the Crystal Palace unguarded. We are low on allies, time is ripping apart, things are popping up everywhere without warning and we need one hell of a plan to pull this off. Which we don't have."

"I have an idea." I started toward the apothecary. "At least part of a plan, anyway." I headed inside to enlist the Zulus. I hoped they would be eager to return payback on the Vikings who had murdered their leader. Before I disappeared, I ribbed: "Dodger, you haven't changed a bit."

"Thanks for noticing."

Yes, I was feeling better. Things were perfectly under control. When I returned a few minutes later, she was still there, partly glaring at me and partly anxious. She could have left. I think the old Dodger would have. I was glad that she had stayed.

"They'll help?"

"Yes."

"Oh no." She cocked her head to the side.

"What?"

"I can tell by your look that it's a—"

"Terrible idea?"

I'm not sure about you, Ollie. You're not yourself. And I'm not sure about whatever you're gearing up for, either." Edward, Abbey, and Byron lined up and listened in expectantly. "But I still believe in you. And they do too." She nodded. "Let's do it."

"Good." I directed the foundlings to stay put as Dodger and I recovered the steam-cycle. We both hopped on. "Cause you're not going to like it."

Chapter 22
Part of a Plan

"You're right." Dodger lowered her goggles as the steam-cycle raced forward, kicking up loose dirt and mud from the street. "I hate this plan. Didn't we do this already?"

"No, now we're going *back* to the Crystal Palace, it's totally different," I said, yelling to be heard over the roar of the motor and the growl of the dinosaur behind us. I think the Megalosaurus and I were becoming friends. You know, the type one invites over for lunch. "Oh, and we're finally off that street."

Another difference between then and this moment was that it was now nigh impossible to see. Night had swung down on us hard. Gas lamplighters stalked the streets but were warned away from our route, meaning we were plunged into darkness with just the ambient light of the city, the steam-cycle's lone gaslamp headlight, and the hazy glow of the moon as its light diffused through foggy coal-dust clouds.

"That's it," Dodger said. "I come up with the plans from now on."

It had been difficult to lure the beast back. The dinosaur had been sleepy, content, and difficult to rouse. It was, after all, an animal, and most animals liked nothing more than a fresh meal and a good nap. Dodger and I probably could have sat on the thing without it opening an eye. Maybe I'd missed a once-in-a-lifetime opportunity to ride a dinosaur.

Our mission had been further thwarted by Bucket's Peelers, who had done an admirable job of overturning carriages, using mechanical street sweepers, and barricading the borders of the warehouse where the animal slumbered. There were many things that Bucket was skilled in, but he excelled at putting people and things into cages. Those barricades now barred our way, leading to a circuitous route that threatened to derail our plan. We were already short on time.

We had to break open the barricade on the street above the warehouse completely. Even with the gaping invitation, the sleepy critter had no desire to wander this strange new world.

In the end, Dodger and I had to resort to bribery. We improvised a makeshift sled, secured it to the back of the steam-cycle, and tied on a hefty piece of cow, fresh from a butcher's shop. We already knew our beasty liked the taste of beef. Once the smell of blood was in the air and the barricade broken, we had her enticed.

Maybe a little too enticed. With that, the dinosaur snapped just above the cow carcass dragging behind the bike, her drool dripping off her snapping maw.

The Zulus should be waiting at our meet-up point near the Palace, past the gardens where we'd first encountered the dinosaur. It was the wrong end of where we needed to be, but when we met back up with Bucket at the warehouse, he was insistent that we follow our dinosaur's previous path since those streets were already wrecked, barricaded, and "they're already familiar to her," he'd argued.

"I don't think that's a problem," I told him. So, here we were. I also suspected that the foundlings would meet us somewhere along our route because of course they would. One of these days, I would need to have a talk with Edward about that.

"How are we doing on time?" she asked, snapping me back to the moment.

I caught sight of the hands of a nearby steam-powered clock. Just under an hour left. "We're running fashionably late."

"Right on time, then." She pressed down on the gear shift and the steam-cycle shot ahead. Unbelievably, our dinosaur kept up. It was either a game to her or she really wanted her late teatime. We probably should have come up with a name for her. I was about to suggest Victoria, after the Queen, when Dodger asked, "Do you think they'll let us in the Palace without tickets?" as if Dodger had queued or ever purchased admission before. Of course, the normally buzzing Palace was closed until further notice or *until the end of time.*

I checked back on our chomping dinosaur. Her eyes were seemingly hungry for anything she could clamp down on with her vice-like jaws. "I think we have our ticket."

"I can't wait to see the Vikings' faces."

As we flew by the streets of Westminster, past Parliament, evidence of the time distortion warped around us. The Clock Tower, long under construction, was now complete. I had heard earlier that it had disappeared. But now, it was back and finished. A large clock face loomed above us, hands pointed at eight o'clock. Reverberating bells rang out. Victoria rumbled in response, clearly annoyed. Me too. I hoped that clock wasn't set on becoming a permanent fixture of London.

An ugly building appeared out of nowhere. I had no idea how something could be built so large. It reached high into the sky, cylindrical, wide in the middle and narrowing into a tip at the top. Black and white glasses spiraled around the building. It was as if someone, maybe an artist who really liked giant gherkins, had decided to outdo the Crystal Palace.

"What the bloody hell is that?" Dodger asked. "It looks like a giant egg."

I disagreed. It made the Palace anodyne by contrast. See, I used another big word, Pip. The future was full of intriguing things. That being considered, I preferred the simpler buildings of the past.

We plowed ahead, Dodger at the wheel, powerless to stop the strings of time from unraveling as our present became entangled with both the past and the future. We drove by an alarmingly large and smelly orange-red salamander-looking thing that was as tall as a hogshead and as long as a carriage bus.

It seemed disinterested in us and luckily, our dinosaur was just as impartial, preferring the taste it had already experienced versus a creature that smelled of sewage. The giant salamander smelled as if it had crawled out of the bottom of the Thames.

Dodger and I held our noses.

"This is only going to get worse," I said, nasally.

"And we're outgunned," she answered. "The Peelers have their work cut out for them. I don't think they'll make it to the Palace to lend a hand."

"We have the Zulus and this lovely beasty back there. Let Brownlow's mercenaries deal with our dinosaur for a change while we find a discrete way to slip inside."

"You're lucky you didn't push me away too," Dodger admonished. "I know a way in."

Before long, we reached the familiar greens of the Exhibition grounds. Ahead of the main entrance of the Crystal Palace, looking burly and mean, were Brownlow's Vikings. They were numerous and dangerous enough to stop anything from getting inside.

Almost anything. Maybe I should have called our Megalosaurus *Grendel* instead. I couldn't see the Vikings' faces well, even those caught in our headlight, but I imagined them wide-eyed and slacked-jawed. The dark night and fog cut both ways. The only indications that we were on them were the increasing thrum of our steam-engine and the stomping of our dinner guest. "Get ready," I said.

"I'm ready, *you* get ready," she kicked the engine of the steam-cycle into its highest gear. It lurched forward into the Vikings. They broke formation as she bailed off the bike.

I jumped too, but not as gracefully. We hit the greens hard, tucked and rolled away, colliding against each other. We stopped soon after, slowed by the entangling of our bodies and the tall, thankfully soft, uncut grass. Every part of my body let me know I was an idiot. But at least I was an *alive* idiot. For now.

"Ow." I said, trying to de-pretzel myself from Dodger. I tried to reorient myself so that I could see the Vikings, but my head spun.

"Oh, I'm going to feel that in the morning," Dodger said, wincing while separating herself from me.

"What do you mean in the morning? I feel it now."

But she looked in worse shape than I did. Her jacket was in tatters. She reached inside it to retrieve her glass flask. It had a large crack in it and its contents ran out over her hands. The cold, askew glance she gave me could have frozen a roaring fireplace.

But our ploy had worked. The steam-cycle had plowed into the Vikings as our improvised Grendel growled. She stood before them as if deciding whether to take her flank steak dinner from the sled or to take a bite out of the Viking moveable feast.

One of the Vikings shouted a word that sounded like, "Monster!"

The Viking chief answered angrily, *"Eldhúsfífl."*

I didn't know what it meant, but I could tell the large Norseman was unhappy with our surprise visit. Before the dinosaur decided from its menu options and the Vikings could regroup, the chanting, rushing whoops of our Zulu allies were on them, followed by sharp spears out and ready to serve up Norse-on-a-stick. It all had happened so fast, precisely as planned, that I was equally surprised.

Our dinosaur made her decision. She found the cow carcass, snatched it within her jaws, lifted her cavernous head high and swallowed it whole. Sated, she once again stomped away as the Zulus engaged the muddled Vikings. The night air erupted into a clattering of swords and spears. The ground shook with the steps of the dinosaur and our chance to sneak in the building was now. "Time to go."

"Follow me," Dodger said. And I did, creeping through the night and along the dewy gardens on the way inside the Crystal Palace to confront my former father.

Chapter 23
Coelophysis

It was brighter inside the Crystal Palace than I expected. While there were no lit gaslamps and the moonglow couldn't stretch inside here, light from unknown sources flickered, sparks flew randomly from some sort of electric display, and an ill glow of purple and blue swept across the floor.

I traced the colors to a large glass orb that crackled with thin tendrils that streaked inside like lightning. It was fascinating to watch, but also hard on my eyes. I blinked the brightness away and was plunged back into shadow.

Something moved. Dodger stilled. I couldn't see anything thanks to light blindness. There was movement of shadows and a clank on the floor. I stopped breathing. We were unarmed, relying strictly on stealth. And we had a long way to go to reach the other side of the Palace. We didn't have time to spare.

"You can come out now." I took a gamble, guessing that the clatter belonged to a few small allies.

"I think they heard us." A familiar voice answered.

Edward stepped out of the shadows. Abbey and Byron revealed themselves too.

"Children," I said, bidding my heart to beat normally. "What are you doing here? You were supposed to stay behind, keep safe, not be here in the building where all the danger is."

"We're children," Edward answered. "We don't listen."

"I blame you, Dodger."

"What? I listen to the rules just fine, I choose to ignore them," she said. "Children, listen to Oliver. Scoot outside, the lot of you."

"It's dangerous out there too," Byron had his speech prepared. "We was minding our own business behind these crates and that giant beast ran by. It didn't pay us any attention, but it could have."

"Those men outside are scary," Abbey added. "And so is that big monster. I wanna stay with you."

"You weren't supposed to leave the apothecary," is what I wanted to say to correct them, but I knew this was going to happen so instead I heard myself say, "Stay close."

They'd likely headed over to the Palace the second Dodger and I had gone down to collect the dinosaur. World's best caregiver, right here. Edward was still nursing his injured arm.

"Change of heart?" Dodger carefully made her way forward.

"Something you said earlier, about sticking together." I probably shouldn't have pushed Pip away either. My anger toward him had melted. It would have been nice to have his smarts here. Maybe he could have explained what that purple lightning in the glass globe was.

Abbey touched the glowing orb with her fingertips. The purple lightning gravitated toward her fingers. She giggled. "It tickles."

"That thing really takes the egg," Byron said wide-eyed.

Edward kneeled next to the ball. "This wasn't on before." It made sense, you wouldn't see it well during the day, but that also meant that there was power on in the Palace – we were on the right track. Brownlow was here, somewhere.

"Children, that's the opposite of sticking close and staying safe." They reluctantly pulled away from the strange device as we plunged deeper inside.

***

As my vision returned and objects bumped back into place, I realized where we were and why I had thought of Pip: We were underneath the catwalks where we had met earlier. What had seemed like a lifetime ago had only been a late lunch.

In the intervening space since the Megalosaurus attack, the catwalks had collapsed, exhibits were overturned, glass walls were shattered or cracked, and the floors were filled with the rubbish of the fleeing crowd.

I knew what was around us. Dinosaur skeletons stretched into view. Looking up at them, the fossils appeared more mammoth than before. While I had been able to see all of them from my perch with Pip above, from below, I couldn't even get one into my field of vision.

I think the fossilized remains in front of me belonged to that of the long neck and tail that was put together with the gears and pulleys I'd seen earlier. They had enabled the dinosaurs to 'move' when the Crystal Palace had been operational. Now, the ropes sagged and the gears were still, awaiting the spark of life that would animate them once more.

It was sobering and perhaps a little scary to think that these behemoths could not survive this hostile universe. What chance have we, being so small and prone to destruction ourselves?

Movement and a clatter of sounds snapped my attention to the corner. Shadows and darkness were all that I saw but I could have sworn I heard the melodic chirping of a bird. "Did anyone else hear or see anything?"

"Probably some pigeons flew in." Edward answered. "With the windows broken, they can fly in and out as they like."

A chittering came not from the corner as before but in front of us. Flashes of purple light hindered our vision. We weren't alone in here, but my heart settled knowing that it was likely small and harmless. "They didn't have to scare us like that."

"Us? I happen to like birds," Dodger reminded me. "It was a sweet thing you did for me, Ollie. I never thanked you for that."

I nodded. Once, a long time ago, I'd left an automaton bird for her, a replacement that had been destroyed by the Old Man when we were both children. I'd never heard anything about it until now. I wondered if that had helped fuel her change, and what other small acts and things had added to that. People don't turn 180 degrees overnight (unless you were Scrooge). It normally took a long and winding path full of missteps. But the journey to change *could* be made.

"Well, we're here, at the dinosaur exhibit. That means we need to go this way," Edward pointed out. It seemed such a short distance in theory, but my gut told me it wouldn't be so easy.

"How much time do we have left?" I asked. Telling time without my timepiece was proving complicated.

"Eight-thirteen," Dodger answered, snapping a pocketwatch closed. I gave her a wry look. Dodger didn't have a timepiece. "What? Found it on the floor, mate." I'm sure she did. Likely, that floor had been someone's pocket. "Thought it might come in handy to know the time given that we only have twenty-seven minutes to stop Brownlow."

We headed the way Edward pointed, quickening our stride and dodging debris. In the crowds from earlier, it would have taken hours to squeeze through. Now, our two-minute crossing was only delayed by darkness, the intermittent flashes of light, and the random, multitudinous displays and exhibits of the Crystal Palace.

"Oh, that's neat," Abbey said. Ahead of her was a stuffed bird. It had a long and slender neck, like a goose but if a goose was twice as tall. The creature's wings were more like feathery arms that ended in talon claws. It had blue plumage, but the rest of its body, except for the matching blue tips of its long whiplike tail, was as black as a crow.

The lights continued to flicker. Somehow, the creature seemed to have moved closer. I saw another one on our left as if it had appeared from out of the shadows. The display was blocking our progress. Had it always been there? I didn't remember it from before. They looked awfully realistic—

It blinked.

Strange. Taxidermied animals didn't do that. Was it made to move like the steam-powered dinosaurs on display? My gut told me no—

"Abbey, watch out," I called. But it was too late. The creature leaped out into the air, talons-first. She shrieked and tried to dodge its pounce, but it latched onto her.

"That's no bird." I ripped the creature off her. It was surprisingly light, but I thought it must have been another dinosaur, a smaller relative of our giant friend outside. It snapped at me, its narrow jaw revealing sharp teeth. I tried to hold it back, but I earned a few nips. As I winced away the sudden sharp stabbing needles, I realized that it was just trying to defend itself.

The other one jumped at Byron. He swatted it away, but it kept coming. Edward placed himself in front of the others, waving his good arm around to make himself more threatening. The creature started to back away, calling in alarm, until another bird-like dinosaur flocked over. The trio advanced with their plumages pulled back and their bodies puffed up.

"Help them," I called to Dodger. But she was dealing with her own creature, nipping at her fingers. I counted five of the overgrown geese encircling us including the one thrashing about in my hands. It kept trying to nip me, flapping its wings wildly, like a goose gone mad. Abbey screamed.

The dinosaur flapped in a frenzy until it tore free of my hands. It ruffled its feathers and joined its flock, turning back on us. Abbey fled toward the safety of Dodger, who shielded Edward and Byron from the four dinosaurs. The fifth darted toward an upturned table and perched on it, gaining a height advantage on us. They were fleet-footed, agile, and cunning little devils.

Purple light continued to flicker on and off. I could only see in short bursts and then all would go black. One moment, a dinosaur would be in one spot, the other, gone completely, only to show up in a place I wasn't expecting.

"I've already avoided being eaten once today," Dodger said. "And I'd like to keep those earlier efforts from being in vain."

"Me, too."

"Same," Edward said. "My sleeve was in its jaws."

The creatures pressed us into the animatronic fossils. We were surrounded by dinosaurs, backed against bones, as five angry murder-geese closed in. They chirped and nipped at each other as if to communicate that dinner was ready.

With claws out and jaws open, the dinosaurs readied to pounce.

Chapter 24
Pip and Pocket

The cueball crashed into the triangle of billiards with a satisfying crack. The solid seven sunk into the corner left pocket. The cracking and sinking of the balls in the newer American game of pool was much more cathartic to Pip and Pocket than snooker or English billiards could ever be. Unfortunately, they only had those carom-style tables at their social club, The Finches of the Grove.

That's why they'd sprung for the red felt and solid oak table, squeezing it into their overly stuffed dining room – bachelors like themselves didn't need a set place to eat anyway.

"Something on your mind, Pip?" Pocket asked as he waited, resting on his cue stick, for his turn. Pip took a shot at another solid, the ball rocketing away and ricocheting the length of the table. "What did that fiver ever do to you?"

"End of the world stuff." Pip answered, edging to the side of the room where a China cabinet pressed against the cracking plaster wall.

"Strange days in London, yeah?" Pocket took a wild shot and watched as his stripe miraculously rolled in. "I heard about your dinosaur, but that isn't the strangest happening by far." He stood, leaning against the cue, the game momentarily forgotten as he told his tale.

"I was at the Commons, discussing business with the MPs, when a cry went up from outside the chambers. We all went out, in orderly fashion, to see that the whole of the unfinished Clock Tower was gone, scaffolding and all. You recall, where they were fixing to hang Big Ben?"

"I pray you're talking about the bell rather than a person?"

"Her Majesty came out from Buckingham later to see for herself. Though I couldn't catch an audience with the Queen." Pocket grinned. "Wouldn't that be something?"

"The Queen, the city, everything, Pocket," Pip said with a note of finality, "I'm done with it. We need to leave."

"Come now, Pip," Pocket said playfully, "this place has given us so much. It's not like you to jest."

"I'm serious. Brownlow is cracked. Oliver has rejected my offer of partnership; I think I want to go back to the moors. Make amends with my uncle."

"Your uncle has only ever wanted to see you happy," Pocket said, leaning against a sturdy bookcase. "And what about the girl you met, what's-her-name, uh, Estella?"

Pip froze as the question rolled around in his brain. His eyes darted around with uncertainty. He tried to take an unsteady shot but he scratched instead.

"She's lovely," Pip managed to squeak out.

"So, what's the matter?"

"I'm a poor judge of character." Pip placed the cue on the table and squared off against his friend. Or the man he thought was a friend. Was this what Oliver had felt? Suddenly, he understood their falling out much better. "I never mentioned a girl, and I most certainly did not give you her name."

Pocket's expression squared and his face drained of color. After what appeared to be a moment of deliberation, like a judge taking a deep breath before delivering a harsh sentence, Pocket held the cue stick out as a truncheon. "Remember how, when we first met, I made you cry?"

Pip nodded. "I remember. I said I'd never cry again."

"That's a promise you're about to break."

Pocket set out to strike him with the stick, but Pip preemptively lunged at the weak wooden middle. The cue snapped into two at the joint. Pocket threw the sticks down and dove headfirst, knocking Pip onto the billiard table.

Pocket pummeled Pip, striking him in the face with several heavy blows. From underneath, there was little Pip could do but stretch his hand over in hopes of reaching the eight-ball beyond his fingertips.

"It figures you're in his pocket," Pip said.

"With his money, the whole city is. We all are, you included."

Pip pawed at the ball, it spun away at first but then bounced off the cue ball and rolled into his palm. With a yell, he brought the ball up into Pocket's temple, sending him passing out onto the table.

Pip stood, brushing himself off and poking at what would surely be more bruises. Examining his former friend, he said, "Not me, not anymore."

Before leaving, Pip went to a safe hidden behind a framed reproduction of a bare-breasted lady holding the French flag and withdrew a large leather bag. He didn't bother to shut the safe, nor did he take any of the piles of notes stacked neatly inside. But he did replace his hat. A moment later, he took his coat, a bowler, and his leave, slamming the door on the cluttered apartment in a final bid farewell.

Chapter 25
To The Rescue

I didn't know how to get past these dinosaurs. Dodger and I braced as they prepared their pounce. There were five of them, and five of us. We could hardly outrun them all and time was wasting. They formed a semi-circle around us of puffed black feathers that disappeared in the flickering light. Heads bobbed and jerked as they plotted their next move. Their ringleader, on top of the overturned table, squawked orders.

They seemed off, though, as if they were yipping dogs with more bark and less bite, or a murder of crows pushing out a flock of pigeons over a dropped streetside order of fish n' chips. It didn't mean these beasts here lacked bite, but if they wanted us for lunch, I think they would have eaten us by now. Perhaps they wanted something else?

"Any ideas?" Dodger asked.

"I thought dinosaur wrangling was your job." I made sure the three children were tucked away neatly behind us. Abbey kept trying to poke her head out in curiosity. "I was along for the ride."

"That was for the last one," she answered. "These critters are yours."

"Oh, in that case, no, I have no idea at all."

A hissing erupted from the floor of the Palace. It wasn't a snake, and it didn't come from the dinosaurs either. It was mechanical, like the release of pressure in pipes. As the sound grew in strength, I realized that it was from a steam-valve. Someone else was here and they were trying to turn on the dinosaur displays.

The noise caught the attention of our captors too. When a mechanical clanking began the big one jumped haphazardly at the strange and sudden noise. I had the misfortune of being in the ringleader's wayward path, with its teeth exposed and claws out, but it looked like none of this was part of its plan. It was of little consolation to me. With those claws and corrugated teeth my insides would soon be joining my outsides.

A tail lashed out. A giant, skeletal appendage thumped into the creature, sending the smaller dinosaur sailing. It landed with a thud on the wooden floor as the steam-powered animatronics jerked into operation.

The critters scattered as the Camarasaurus waved its tail and moved its neck. The Megalosaurus skeleton snapped its jaws. And the armored Hylaeosaurus jumped to life in jerky movements. They operated as I had seen before, but more noisily as their clicks and gears and pulleys were no longer competing against a cacophonic crowd.

The click and hum of giant glass bulbs hummed as their filaments began to glow. It was the only building in London outfitted with these new electric lights. I'd read in the paper about large faraday discs being used experimentally to illuminate the Crystal Palace at night with electric light to keep the exhibition open later and to show off the world's newest technology. Until now, I didn't think lightbulbs would last, but they proved to be a bright idea.

As impressive as the light was, ironically, it made it hard to see the figure that had appeared on a platform. The figure said, "I'd ask you if you missed me, but I don't think I was gone that long."

"You're right," I said, relieved. My anger had dissipated since our quarrel. Besides, he'd saved my life. "But what made you come back?"

"I had to see who would win in a fight. Looks likes robots to me."

"Does it still count if they're dinosaur robots?" I nodded my head in silent appreciation.

"Boys." Dodger shook her head. "Bloody well get down here."

Pip obliged and came down from the maintenance platform to join our assemblage but chided us with, "You know you're at the wrong end of the Palace, right?"

"Yeah," I said. "We might have not had the greatest plan ever." We still had to get through this wing, cut through the lobby, and enter Brownlow's lair. "What happened?"

"I was playing pool," he said. "And sank a Pocket."

I didn't know what that meant. But as we hurried from our end of the wing toward the arboretum in the middle, he confessed. "I had an uncle who loved me. There was a girl from the Moors I could have married, I'm sure. I could have had a life there, but Brownlow blinded me to that, offered me wealth and more books than I could shelve. I need to prove that I wouldn't make that choice again." He paused for a moment before recanting. "Maybe the books. I do like the books."

Pip was the person I might have become with only a small twist of fate. He bid us to stop and handed me the leather case he'd been carrying. "I brought you this."

I took the case and opened it. Inside was a new set of clothes. But not just any clothing.

"I was serious about the partnership. I believe in the Orphan. I believe in you."

It was a long leather frock coat, black and sturdy, as if designed to take a beating and maybe save me a few bruises too. With it was a midnight-blue scarf. I'd long since lost mine, but the foundlings had noticed that many shops had been sold out across the city. It had become somewhat of a statement.

Dodger looked our way, "Did you bring anything for me? Anything? I could use a new flask."

Pip handed her his, which she drank from greedily, before spitting some out. "Gin, it's always gin."

I put a brotherly hand on Pip's shoulder, shed my tattered jacket, and replaced it with the new one. It fit perfectly as if he'd gotten my measurements by magic. So, this was what tailor-made felt like. As good as it felt though, I thought as I wrapped the scarf around my neck, it didn't feel nearly as good as putting my anger into the past and joining forces together.

"Well, I don't have everything you have, Oliver," Pip confessed as we hurried to the other side of the room. "You can't have everything until you have someone to care about, someone who, for instance, was also swayed by Brownlow." I knew very well he meant Stella. "And I think you're no different. You weren't looking for wealth and means, you weren't looking to be like me. You were looking for connection."

"Perhaps." I answered, eyeing Dodger. I knew full well what Pip was on about. But I hadn't decided how I felt about her.

My look was either lost on Dodger or she chose to deflect. Snapping at us, she said after another swig, "You two, stop your cobbering, we're almost out of time."

"Right."

We made it to the end of the wing. The dinosaurs were still around, chirping, speeding through the wreckage of the Palace, making sure we didn't get too close to whatever it was that they seemed to be guarding. But with the room illuminated, they were a little more skittish around us and instead busied themselves by bobbing their heads and making intimidating noises while ruffling their feathers. I guessed that they still wanted something, but what it was, I didn't know.

Our path through the rubble gave way to a set of wooden doors that opened into the arboretum. Without further hesitation, I swung open the nearest door and stepped through, not knowing what to expect on the other side. I knew enough not to expect it to be deserted, and I was not disappointed. But I didn't expect her.

"Honestly, I expected you to enter through the main doors." A familiar feminine voice called out from the shadows of the darkened botanical gardens. She stepped out and said, "You're in the wrong wing, you know."

"Yeah, I thought we'd take Brownlow by surprise," I said, as we stopped to confront Stella once more. My shoulders slumped and my heart raced. There wasn't time for this. "But I see the flaw in that now."

"Guys," Dodger reminded us. "No time, start fighting."

"Well then, enough chatter," she said. "Dodger and I agree." From behind her, hidden within the shadows of the elms, pulses of red energy fired.

Chapter 26
Tick-Tock

An elm under glass. As if London had the power to bottle nature itself. Tall, thick trees grew within the high arched glass canopy. Neatly trimmed hedges, plants and shrubs of all sorts lined wooden walks. But the centerpiece of all this was a tree so tall and majestic that the Palace was literally built around it, as if it was just another grand exhibition piece on display.

However, the trees – the giant elm in particular – made for fantastic cover. This arboretum was to our benefit, a greenhouse full of make-shift fortifications. We all dove in separate fashion behind the relative safety of thick trunks in the groves as the shooting started.

Pip and I found ourselves huddled behind a particularly wide trunk. I noted that, where the red beam struck, short bursts of flame followed. Being shot at was one thing, but I did not want to burst into fire one bit.

"Oh, immolation, how quaint," Pip said. I think that was his way of agreeing.

The shooting stopped for a moment. "Thanks for the wild goose chase, by the way," Stella said as the crackle of smoldering tree bark and wooden doors subsided. "The children weren't there, of course, so it was nice of you to bring them with you. Not smart, but nice."

I followed the sound of her voice as she moved in search of us. "It wasn't a total loss," she continued, "I found a cute outfit. Your ghostly friend Nell has an amazing Curiosity Shop."

Stella had indeed changed, in more ways than one. But in the literal sense, I'd briefly caught a glimpse of her new attire. She now wore a dark pleated skirt, a frilly white top with a black corset and brass fasteners over the shoulders. "Despite you trying to kill us," Pip called out, "you do look quite lovely."

"What are you doing?" I belted out in hushed rebuke.

"Sorry, it's true," Pip mouthed, as Stella found us.

"Why thank you, Pip, you're sweet. But I'm not trying to kill anyone, I just need to delay you for," she pulled out that rectangle contraption again, it really was an updated pocket-watch, "another twenty minutes." She placed one hand akimbo and used the other to direct whatever it was that had fired at us. Two humanoid machines, decked out in some sort of translucent hardened material, stalked out from the shadows.

"Now those are robots," Pip said. "I think."

"Got any dinosaurs around?" I gulped.

Our cover disappeared as a bright red flash made kindling of our tree. Splinters sprayed over us as we ducked down. After it stopped raining matchsticks, I saw that the trunk was charred around the area that had been blown out. With chunks that large, nowhere was safe anymore, we had to take these machines head on. But how?

That's when I noticed Dodger in the trees above us. She was slowly making her way above the robot on our right – or her right, our left – nevermind. She needed a bit more time. "So, Stella," I began, as I stood with my hands up. I kicked Pip hard enough so that he'd do the same. "How does someone capture your heart? I'm asking for a friend."

"Mr. Twist!" Pip gave me a look that could kill, replete with red cheeks. Turning to Stella sheepishly, he said, "I mean, since he asked—"

Dodger dropped onto the machine, colliding with it as it spun around to meet its attacker in vain. Her ambush must have set off a defense mechanism, because it fired. But the red beam went wild, firing not into Dodger but into its companion instead, as Dodger kicked the weapon hard. The other robot's midsection erupted in showers of sparks. It collapsed on the ground, into a metal heap.

It wasn't over yet. The ruined robot's weapon also fired, but it shot at its attacker, like a last salvo before being destroyed by friendly fire. Their defense systems had worked against each other. Just like the tree from earlier, Dodger's robot exploded from the volley into a smoking husk, with Dodger going down with it. I was worried there for a second but, like an alley cat, she landed on her feet.

"Two for one, Dodger, you're getting rusty," I said as we made our move.

"I know, I know," she said, extricating herself from the wreckage, "I should have gotten Stella, too. Sloppy."

"Edward, head into the gardens, get the others to safety," I called. Three children emerged from the bushes.

"Do we have too?" Abbey asked.

"Go," I barked. I could barely see their outlines, but I could tell they understood my urgency this time as Edward, Byron, and Abbey raced deeper into the arboretum.

There were no electric lights in this part of the Palace. Instead, there were unlit candles and gaslamps scattered throughout. The children would be safer there, I hoped, hidden among the foliage of the indoor gardens. My biggest shock came from the fact that they had listened.

Pip and I joined Dodger as she recovered from her aerial acrobatics. The three of us ignored Stella and headed past her as the two robots smoked and sparked.

"You think that's it?" We all turned back to face Stella's taunt. She plucked my timepiece out from a pocket in her new outfit. Nell liked pockets so she sewed them into all her clothing. Stella must have liked that too. "I have your watch, Oliver. I can turn back time and start again. I have all night while you only have minutes."

She was right, of course. This was a losing game. My stomach lurched to the floor. I didn't know how we were going to win this. With a flair-ish flick of her wrist, the watch popped open.

I readied for a swirl of copper that I'd never remember. All I'd know is that the robots would be standing over me, Dodger would likely miss her mark because of Stella's foreknowledge and all three of us would soon be blasted to bits while Brownlow won unchecked.

Stella smiled. "I told you that you were on the losing side."

I braced for the clock to reset, but—

Nothing happened.

"How does this thing work?" Stella shook the watch. "It's not like the stupid map, is it? Nothing works right here."

I relaxed my stiffened shoulders. This wasn't like before when Dodger had stolen my watch and used it against me. Now, I realized I had help on the inside. The literal inside. Of the watch.

Nell.

"It's supposed to work for anybody, right?" Dodger asked.

"Unless someone is breaking the rules for us," I said, knowingly.

"Right-o," Pip said. "Must be your ghosty friend, aye?"

Stella slunk down. Nell's voice piped out of the watch. "Judging by how poorly you lot are doing without me, Oliver, I was not going to let her jump back in time, no matter the consequences."

"Well," I breathed out, "We could sure use your help."

"Oliver, I can stop Brownlow, all you have to do is get me—"

Stella snapped the watch closed. "Okay, things are going off script. That's what improv classes are for."

"Forget it, Stella, you've had your chance and you've lost. The children are safe, and it's the four of us against you now. Help us stop Brownlow, give me the watch," I begged.

She seemed to consider it for half a second before a mechanical hand swatted me aside. I flew back some way until I landed onto soft underbrush. I was thankful that it wasn't the trunk of a tree or I likely wouldn't have gotten back up. And luckily, my spiffy new frock coat absorbed some of the blow. Thanks, Pip.

It took me a dizzying moment to figure out what had happened. One of the robots must not have been as badly damaged as I'd thought or it somehow had repaired itself. It had charged at me while I was distracted by Stella. My head swam like it had been tossed in the Thames. My vision was blurry.

It took me a moment to gather my bearings, but in the meantime, I saw what I thought was a shadowy robed figure standing before me.

Why was there a shadowy robed figure staring at me? Wasn't there enough going on?

I expected it to poke a bony finger at me when I realized who it was. My heart skipped a beat. I waited a moment to make sure it beat again so that I was sure I wasn't dead, because that's usually how one saw our uninvited and unexpected guest.

The shadowy robed figure was the Spirit of Christmas Future, or better known as . . .

Death.

Now what?

Chapter 27
The Fate of the Future

Death stood stone-still before me.

I had seen it before. It had chilled me then and it chilled me now. A black hood shadowed its face but it was short with a slender frame, no taller than I. The most peculiar thing about the figure was that, instead of a scythe, or skeletal fingers prodding one to an opened grave it was . . .

Knitting?

It couldn't have been knitting, it was too absurd. I'd been smacked in the head too hard. Yet I distinctly saw it knitting.

A cold voice spoke to me and every bit of my skin crawled and tingled. The form of Death disappeared.

I wondered if others had seen it, or if I was the only one. Had it spoken to the others too?

The words it spoke to me had been as confusing as the apparition itself. It spoke of a warning. Consequences. Deaths of those I cared about. It was too much, I shook the words out of my head, none of what it had said would matter anyway if we didn't stop Brownlow.

But the situation looked as grim as the Reaper itself.

Stella was unsettled. There was no way to know if she had seen or heard it, too, but I had no time to think on it further. There wasn't much time left.

Ahead, the robot started attacking Pip and Dodger after it had smacked me senseless. Right. Stop the robot. Get past Stella, save the world. I dusted off my new frock coat Pip had brought me and got right back to it.

Of everything going on, my focus had to be on shutting Brownlow down. I had to let Pip and Dodger deal with the murder-bot. Dodger kicked it but that didn't stop it. Pip punched it and held his hand while wincing with pain. The robot rose higher, smoke still pouring from its absent belly, and yet it easily deflected their attacks, but I had to leave Pip and Dodger to it, I hoped they would understand.

I slunk off and approached the corridors that would lead me into the East Wing, Stella stopped me. I thought about throttling her or pushing past her, but she still looked shaken and not at all as menacing as before.

"What's wrong?"

"Dddid you see it?" she asked. Her hands were trembling. "I h-heard it in my h-head. A voice. Cold as the wind. I saw her. A woman knitting." So, she had seen it too. "Who, um, what was that?"

"It's the very essence of Fate," I explained. I saw that she didn't understand. "Where Nell is the beginning, Death is the end."

"Death?" She said, "As in the Reaper?"

I nodded, eyeing the room past her. I could leave her now, and I knew she wouldn't stop me. But I've always had a hard time with the idea that I couldn't save everyone. I had to try. Stella wasn't evil, she could still swing our way. "What did it say to you?"

"The voice told me," Stella eyed the arboretum as if eyes were watching her. "She told me I would die here," she gulped, "I don't want to die, please," she pulled at my coat, "don't let me die."

"Listen to me," I took her by her shoulders, "no one else is going to die here. Not you, not anyone, not Pip, not the children. We can stop this. We can stop Brownlow. Together. But first, give me my watch."

Tears ran down her cheeks. They briefly reminded me of her acting prowess and how she had fooled us before. But I didn't think this was an act. She was coming around. And if we *all* stood together against him, as Nell had instructed, there might be a chance . . .

Before she could respond the building began to rattle. The wooden floorboards creaked and rattled below. Above, the high arched windows shook. Trees began to sway. Iron buckled, it groaned in a grotesque whine as the metal frame buckled and bent. Panes of glass cracked, shattered, dropping deadly shards.

Stella and I ducked underneath the nearest archway and covered our faces. This was not another earthquake. It must have been from Brownlow's time-machine, as if it was trumpeting the end.

From a few meters away, Dodger and Pip were taken off balance. The robot moved in, unfazed, and smacked Dodger to the ground with a thud that could be heard over the collapsing Palace. The machine stood in triumph over the two, readying killing blows.

The sky quieted. The shaking stopped. Broken glass never reached us. It was calm, cool, airy, and dark.

The entirety of the Crystal Palace had vanished.

***

It was gone. One moment, we were standing in the world's most expansive plate-glass and cast-iron exhibition center and the next moment, we were all standing in an open field. Verdant hills of green, dark in the night sky, rolled out across my night-blind vision. It was as if the Crystal Palace had never existed.

Movement is what pulled my eye. Dodger and Pip were still being attacked by the robot, but the shift in scenery seemed to have bought them some time as the robot processed the impossible. The Zulus and Vikings fought each other across the manicured lawn and concrete steps leading to nothing. From what I could tell, the too few numbers of the Zulu warriors were losing against the rage of the Viking horde.

And the children were likely far back in the groves of trees beyond my sight, since the trees had been there long before the building. Out of all of them, they were the safest.

The Megalosaurus growled from a distance not-so-distant. Where the West Wing had been was now a grassy slope which eased downward to where the Zulus and Vikings clashed.

From beside us came the sound of flapping wings and beating claws. I was confused until I saw the bird-like dinosaurs stampeding directly toward me. Blue snouts and upturned head quills poked above the rise, quick and bird-like, away from the sound of the Megalosaurus and the fighting, as if running toward something. Something worth protecting.

I looked to Dodger and Pip, who needed the most immediate help. As quick as I could, I took off my frock coat, and raced closer to the pair, leaving a still-shocked Stella to herself. Waving my new coat around, yelling and screaming, I did my best to redirect the geese-sized dinosaurs away from me and toward them. I'm sure Dodger wasn't too happy with that, but a moment later, she understood what I was doing. She elbowed Pip and they both began to yelp excitedly.

Chaos did the trick. The only safe path through the trees (but away from the strange, whooping humans) was *through* the robot. They executed a sharp left turn, almost in unison, which brought them into the path of the machine.

Pip and Dodger dove away as the five deadly dinosaurs raced by. The leading couple leapt onto the robot, plucked at several exposed wires and leapt off. The head of the robot sparked where its mechanical red eye used to be. The pair kept going in the direction of the children. Two more slammed into the machine, knocking it down. They bit and clawed the gaping hole left by the other robot's laser blast. Claws screeched on metal as the last one, smaller than the others, pounced harmlessly into the threat and raced on its harried way, as if mimicking its flock.

The robot sputtered. Sparks flew as it joined its brother for hopefully the last time.

Even though the dinosaurs fled in the direction of the children, I had no way to warn them, I had cleaned up one mess only to create another. I had to trust that the children were far enough away or that Edward could keep them safe, until we could put an end to this madness.

With the immediate crisis averted, I went back to Stella and took her by the elbows to lift her up, checking her over for injuries. I didn't know if any glass from the ceiling had hit her before the building disappeared. "Are you all right?"

She nodded as Dodger and Pip hurried over.

"Score one for the dinosaurs. It's all tied one-one now," Pip said. "Who would've believed?"

"Glad I wasn't part of that bet," Dodger said. "What's the pot?"

"Respect," Pip answered. Dodger shook her head, as there was no way she was serving so precious a dish as that. To Stella, he said, "Glad to see we're all back together, and on the same side."

Stella nodded tearfully. But she'd stopped shaking, a good sign.

"Oh, and by the way," Dodger asked, raising her voice, "what the bloody hell happened to the building?"

"It makes sense," Stella whispered quietly. She stepped away, her eyes widening and her head hanging to one side. "It makes sense . . ."

I thought she was still mulling over the words from Fate, but she continued, "This building wasn't here for long. I Googled it before I came through. The Palace was moved after the Expo and later it burned to the ground." Her voice gained confidence the more she explained. "It wasn't here long."

"How does a glass building burn?"

"Wooden floors, flammable exhibits, trees. The glass warped and iron bars bent. Whole thing collapsed." Stella seemed stronger, her foreknowledge putting her back onto more certain ground. Good, we needed her help. That is, if she were truly on our side. None of us could be sure of her loyalties. Aside from Pip.

We all took in the surrounding area again. Hyde Park had returned as I remembered it long before construction began. Not ten foot away was the spot where Mr. Brownlow's fiancée had been murdered. Now that the building was gone, and the glass walls were no more—

"Where is Brownlow?" I asked, my heart sinking. Had we been wrong all along? No time-machine, no Brownlow. Instead, three large Faraday discs enclosed an area about five feet in a triangle. Beyond the generators, there was a single, large spool of copper wire. The thick wire led to a huge coil wrapped around a rectangular object flat, wide, and iron.

"An electric magnet," Pip said. "He used faraday discs to build a massive homopolar generator."

"No wonder everything has gone to blazes. This power-source must be ripping through time," Dodger realized.

In the center of the equipment, dead grass gave an impression of a small sleigh-looking platform, likely belonging to the bottom of the time-machine.

"Where is it?" How could we stop something that wasn't there?

"You're not thinking in terms of time," Pip answered. "He's here. It's a matter of when. Give it a moment."

As if on command, the large discs started to spin. Glass bulbs encircling the field began to burn a glowing vermilion. The time-machine flashed into existence as if it had been there all along.

As the light receded, I saw for the first time Mr. Brownlow's invention. The time-machine had a large rotating clock at the rear, a chair of red velvet in which an aging Mr. Brownlow sat, and a control panel of levers and dials, all surrounded in a maze of bronze and copper pipes, gears, and machinery from a hodgepodge of timelines past, present, and future.

He unfolded from his machine gingerly, taking care with the use of his hooked cane to hobble over to us in no hurry. He checked his silver timepiece, looked up at us to study our faces and said, "Ahh, precisely on time. Thank you for your punctuality."

A whirring sounded as the large clock rotated and flattened out horizontally, as if it had been rigged as a Faraday disc. As it did, the three others spun faster. What Pip had described as some sort of electromagnet, crackled with current. I could feel energy in the air as the hairs on my neck and arms began to rise.

A copper light shot out of the time-machine from above the upturned clock, like a giant gaslamp spotlight, reaching out into the sky. As the discs spun with lightning speed, a wind started to pick up, swirling around us. Our coats began flapping wildly.

The time-machine disappeared.

It was gone for a moment only to reappear. It did it again. And again. And again.

He looked back at the pulsating machine and, answering our unasked questions, explained, "My machine isn't natural, the way your watch works. Every trip my machine takes, it breaks the laws of the universe, if I keep doing it, eventually time itself will break down."

"This won't bring your fiancée back," I pleaded.

"Oh, it does indeed." Brownlow said. "See, I met a man named Einstein, he didn't believe in time-travel, but he did have some interesting theories."

"Oh, great, a monologue," Stella said.

Dodger nodded. "Can we skip to the punching, please?"

"You don't want to hear about photons, then?" Brownlow went on, "How they exist at every moment at once, from birth to death? You see, my plan is quite simple. I'm bringing us into the light."

That didn't make any sense to me, but I didn't know anything about photons or Einsteins, or even time-travel. If Brownlow had meant that everything would exist all at once, like a photon, from birth to death, then our world was about to get a lot more crowded.

"What you're attempting is impossible," Pip said. For once, I was glad that he was smarter than me. "It doesn't work like that."

"You're wrong," Brownlow snapped. "When time stops, everything will exist, altogether, like a light particle. Past, present and future, living together. Long lost loves. No death or decay. I've seen it." He looked at his watch once more and snapped it closed with a flourish and wry smile.

"It's 8:35 p.m. And you're too late to stop me. I know because I've seen that too. You don't stop me, Oliver."

The time-machine continued to phase in and out, faster and faster, the whirlwind whipped us harder and harder. The sky burst with lightning, hazing in the fog, illuminating the night sky. Leaves scattered and raced across my field of vision. Beyond us, the clacking and clanging of weapons continued, and the rumbling of the Megalosaurus added to the swirling light-storm a sound like thunder.

Like a strike of lightning, it all crashed together for me. Something Stella had said about the Crystal Palace had sent gears in my mind turning. The Palace and its grounds had housed the remains of extinct creatures, animals that had lived long before us and for millions of years longer. It explained why so many dinosaurs had appeared and it explained why so many things had disappeared – including the Crystal Palace.

Stella had said it herself. The Palace hadn't lasted long, years at most. Such a short time for so grand a design. It was a pity. There was something else that hadn't been around for very long and would likely not be around much longer.

Humanity.

Humans hadn't existed but mere moments on this planet. Not in the grand scheme of things and not as long as the dinosaurs, I'd read. Humans were fleeting, a single grain in all the sands of the world.

Pip was right. It was impossible to stop time. I saw the flaw in Mr. Brownlow's design. His plan wouldn't work, not the way he foresaw. At the scale of the universe, if everything happened all at once—

From our perspective, time wouldn't stop; *we would*. We would cease to be. We were insignificant in the incomprehensible stretches of time. We would be lost to the chaos and disappear forever.

"My God, he doesn't know." I spoke unconsciously out loud though it was for myself. In the future where he won, he must have only visited a moment, and in the moment, it would have seemed to him like victory. But he didn't stay long enough to see reality collapse around him.

"Moments are fleeting," I said, eyeing Brownlow. "There's so much more than you and I. There's all of us. And even all of us put together are but a blink." I don't think he understood. "Your time-machine will wipe out all of humanity. It'll be like we never existed."

"He's going to kill us?" Pip asked.

"My plan will work as promised, Mr. Twist is engaged in fear-mongering." Brownlow steadied himself on his cane and pulled out a gun. He gave it a weighty feel, as if the weapon had been cursed. An aging, wrinkled hand pointed it at us unsteadily. "As for killing you all, I'm afraid that only one of you will have that pleasure. Let's see, who was it that I was supposed to shoot again?" I couldn't see his eyes move the way they do when recalling a memory, but I could tell by his pause that he was remembering.

"Ah, yes, Stella," he said, taking aim. "I almost forgot."

"What?" Pip asked, his voice frantic and laced with shock.

"What do you mean, me—" Stella said before she was cut off by the report of the pistol.

Mr. Brownlow fired, and Stella flew back.

Chapter 28
Fraying Strands

The Foundlings:

"I'm hungry," Abbey said, holding her tummy. "We haven't eaten all day."

It was a bit of a fib; she had bread and cheese this morning. And Miss Dodger had swiped some chips for her from a cart outside the big glass Palace. Abbey had wiped her greasy fingers off onto her pink and white checkered dress. She still had the stains as proof that she *had* eaten.

But that was before the dinosaur had almost eaten Edward and they had walked forever to end right back at the Palace again. Her feet hurt too. The dress shoes Dodger had picked for her pinched her toes and the buckles bit into her ankles. On top of that, her tummy rumbled again. Rumbling tummies didn't lie, she *was* hungry.

"It's been a long day, Abbey," Edward answered. "I'll find you food, but first we have to help Mr. Twist."

"I'm pretty sure the best way to help is to stay out of the way," Byron warned. Abbey liked Byron's ideas the best. Edward was always getting them into trouble.

"Well, that's not what we're going to do," Edward said matter-of-factly, like a schoolteacher. Abbey hated school; it was boring.

Tall trees and long shadows made it hard for her to see where they were. It was strange that the outside was indoors. Abbey wondered if it was possible to become lost inside of a forest *inside* a building. Before she could think on it longer, the earth began to rumble like her belly, and she fell to the ground, landing roughly on her butt onto wooden flooring.

Ouch. The pain was short lived, however, for the building had disappeared. Questions settled in its place, which masked the aching.

"What happened?" Abbey asked. They were outside again now that the big glass building had gone away. Strange things had been appearing and disappearing all day. She had wished some sweetcakes and strawberries would magically appear, but it was always scary monsters trying to chase her instead. As if on cue, the big beasty from earlier rumbled deeply. She stiffened. "Okay, I'm not hungry anymore."

"Is that what I think it is?" Byron asked.

"Relax, we'll be safe here, stick together." Edward brought Abbey in closer, wrapping his good arm around her. He felt warm against the cool wind that was now moving through the open field since all the walls were gone.

Together, they pressed forward on the path. They'd put some distance between the mean lady and the others already, but now that they were out in the open, even the cover of trees wasn't so safe anymore. Abbey could feel her whole body tremble. It was like last Christmas when the scary spirits had been everywhere. She wished Nell were with them now. She had been a good ghost.

Abbey couldn't imagine it getting much scarier.

The three of them approached a mound in the earth rising between a circle of bushes. It didn't look natural; it looked like creatures made it. Her curiosity took over and she broke free from Edward's arm to take a closer look. When she reached the rim of blackthorn bushes, she saw that it wasn't a single mound, but several. They looked like small volcanoes with sides so steep you could sled down them, which sounded like fun. Just like drawings she had seen in books, each of the three mounds had a hole in the center. She wondered what was in there—

"Abbey, get back," Edward called.

Silly Edward, he was always saying she couldn't do things and then he'd go off and do something daffy himself. He'd return with bruises or scrapes and lectures from Miss Dodger or Mr. Twist.

This was her discovery, and she wasn't going to listen to him telling her to stop. Her tummy stopped rumbling, and she wasn't shaking anymore. She pressed aside the thorny branches and hurried up the nearest mound. This was fun.

A noise from behind caused Abbey to stop and turn around to look. Branches of low growing trees and the bushes on the ground beyond the boys shook wildly. Large broad leaves moved as something bobbed around it. Edward and Byron went still and pale. A creature was in there. And it seemed to be heading directly towards the mounds and Abbey.

"Stay still," Edward said. "Hold your ground until we know what they want."

They? Abbey wondered. Were those dinosaurs back, the ones that were as large as her? Those claws, she remembered, were as big as her hand and as sharp as shears.

A blue-quilled head poked its head out of the bushes and eyed her angrily, as if Abbey had stolen from it. Byron had once given her that same look when she had taken some of his clay marbles. But she hadn't done anything like that here. Honest.

Four more critters scurried out, the same pack as before. Although this time she realized one of them was smaller than the rest and kept its distance from the others. Its feathers weren't as developed. In some places, it was covered in white fuzz. *A baby?*

They puffed out their feathers, approaching the mounds slowly but surely, as if nothing would stop them. The downy baby mimicked the others. Edward and Byron backed up to her, walking up the steep hill backwards, and getting their clothes caught and torn in the brambles. Still, the dinosaurs closed in. They called to each other in high-pitched chirps and scratchy caws.

"What do they want?" Byron asked.

Abbey thought she knew the answer: they wanted to eat her all up. She held onto the boys tightly, as the nearest dinosaur opened its jaw. Its mouth was full of ragged teeth.

But a wiggling from the hole in the mound caught Abbey's attention too. She spared a glance to see several large oval things settled halfway among grass and small branches. Each of the mounds held three or four of the strange objects. And the one closest to her was moving – as if a creature was inside, trying to escape.

"Look," she called to the boys and pointed. They slowly turned and they all saw the same thing. "Eggs. And one of them is hatching."

Edward gulped. "We stumbled into their nest."

***

The Zulus:

Having been taken and raised in part by missionaries, given books by English authors to memorize, including their holy book, Mandla had always been seen by his tribe as more of a thinker than a fighter. While they accepted him and saw his language and negotiating skills as a necessary evil, they'd never made it a point to fully include him. And that separation had extended to military drills and unit training with their shields and spears.

He'd taken it upon himself to practice at early morning hours during the times he used to be awakened by the missionaries for bible study. But studying a weapon by oneself was different than being taught by his tribe. He found, rather quickly, as this foggy, cold, miserable night wore on, that all the book learning and self-study meant nothing to the Viking Chief threatening to cleave Mandla in two.

The Zulus were fewer in number than the Vikings. Two had fallen in battle in their first encounter, including their leader, Solomon, and two more had fallen so far during this second engagement. Mandla was determined not to add his name to the list of their dead. But his prayers – to the white god, and to his ancestors – went unanswered.

As his tribe fought the others, Mandla had found himself squaring off with the Viking Chief. The giant white man's bearskin cloak was absent. Even through the fog, Mandla could see muscled biceps and a broad chest beneath his grey-white torn tunic. Blood was spattered across the man's face. He was sure none of it was the Viking's own.

A rumble began, pausing the standoff between the two warriors. Soon after, the building behind the Viking, the large clear and iron monstrosity that sought to trap even the trees themselves, had vanished. For once, the time distortions or whatever had thrust him and his men here, had done something good. Off in the distance, a showdown was happening, likely between the *mdidi* Englishmen. Oliver Twist had said they were trying to stop it, but to Mandla, fixing what they had broken was typical of the English. Still, this was their only chance to go home to bury their leader.

First, however, was the fight. And the avenging of Solomon's slaughter. Mandla thrust out and upward with his spear. The attack went nowhere as the Viking deflected his spear thrust with his shield. The Viking followed the block by swinging down a worn battle axe – a far cry from the mighty weapon the chief had used earlier. Still, this blade was no less deadly.

Mandla was tall and wiry, and able to sidestep the attack. The Viking pivoted, swinging the axe vertically to close the gap Mandla had left behind. The axe's wide edge almost caught him in the kidney. He poked his *iklwa* at the larger man and almost hit his mark, but the Viking had stepped into a defensive position after his two wild flails had failed.

Emboldened, Mandla pressed his attack, stabbing his spear forward as he had trained those early hours each morning. But a singular soldier thrusting forward, without his fellow warriors at his side blocking and parrying and shielding their advance, did not have the same effect as a lone fighter. He realized that now, as his mistake became clear.

The Viking had feinted. In his defensive stance, he took advantage of Mandla's uncoordinated attack, using his shield to block the spear and with the same motion, delivered a blow with the butt end of his axe upwards into Mandla's chin that sent the Zulu crashing back. With the initiative, the Viking chief brought the blade crashing down. Mandla had no choice but to sloppily block the skull-splitting blow with the wooden handle of his spear. It took the brunt of the attack, splintering his weapon into two like chopped firewood. Mandla staggered and fell on his knees, as the Viking readied another blow.

It couldn't get any worse than this, Mandla knew, as he briefly wondered if this had been how his chief had been killed. He hoped his ancestors would welcome him home. And if the white man's god greeted him instead, then he hoped that he would show mercy and grant him entry to the lands of his forefathers, for Mandla had no interest in an eternity with those he considered his enemy.

The ground shook. But this was not the same as the shaking before the building vanished. This was familiar. The ground shook again, and from the foggy grove of tall, dark elms, the Megalosaurus returned.

It reverberated a hungry growl that beat into Mandla as it stalked beside the two warriors. His stomach tightened and his knees weakened. Between the Viking's axe, or the beasts' teeth, he knew he was dead. Silently, he whispered a final prayer to any god that would listen: he wished to be slain by the Viking's blade. It was a quicker death, he thought, and a better warrior's death than being ripped apart and eaten.

Chapter 29
Eight-Thirty-Six

Four minutes was all the time we had before humanity was lost forever to the vastness of time. But Stella didn't even have that long. She lay gasping for breath in a puddle of her own blood.

"He shot me?" Stella asked, between sucking breaths.

Pip and I ran toward her and knelt, looking over her wound. Her face was panic-stricken, eyes wild as if searching for a solution or a reason why. Her new white shirt was slick with a growing crimson that smelled of copper. Pip tore off his thick frock coat and placed it under her head. As cool as the night air was, beads of perspiration built on her brow. "Put pressure on the wound," I instructed Pip. "Keep her calm."

"I know, I know." Pip placed firm hands on her abdomen to stem the flow of blood. Luckily for her, Mr. Brownlow must have used a small caliber gun. "Shhh, Stella, you'll be okay, you'll be okay."

I could tell he was lying. I turned my own anger to Brownlow, but I didn't have the words to express it. Instead, he spoke as I seethed.

"She couldn't stop talking about you, Pip," Brownlow said, tossing the still-smoking gun aside. "I paid her to make sure you were distracted, but I knew it couldn't last. Oliver infects everyone he's around, blinds them to the truth." Lightning cracked around the equipment, surrounding the perimeter of the time-machine. He stood defiantly in the center of it all with a straight spine and a smug expression.

"The truth is, Pip," Brownlow continued, "you've never had someone taken away from you. You were too young to remember losing your family; they've always been gone. You left your uncle; he never left you. So, you don't know what it's like. Now that you might lose her, I know you'll understand. The only way to save her is for me to see my plans through. If you do, if you stop Oliver, I promise that you'll see Stella again. You can rule this city. You can have everything you've ever wanted."

"Don't listen to him," I pleaded with Pip.

"I'm not," he said, keeping his eyes glued to Stella. "I'm trusting you."

"We'll save her."

"We better." Pip gave me a quick glance of expectation and took Stella's hand. It looked cold, clammy, and small in his. "How much time do we have?"

"Two-and-a-half minutes," Dodger said, clicking her timepiece closed.

"Great, do we have a plan?" Pip asked.

I answered: "Stop Brownlow before time stops."

"Bugger this," Dodger said. "I'm ending this now."

"Dodger, don't," I yelled after her. But it was too late. She charged at Brownlow, making it as far as the first electric arc between two of the large discs before a zap of electricity caught her and flung her back through the air.

She landed roughly, a few feet away, the edges of her coat charred and smoking. There was a buzzing sound in the air and a lingering sizzling smell. She rolled onto her back and groaned loudly.

"See, I'm quite well protected. The power I need to amplify my time-machine also serves to repel meddling."

"Why are you doing this?" I asked him, the man who'd rescued me, raised me, and then had turned utterly evil. "Why did you shoot her?"

"To save the world, son," He turned away again, putting his back to me. "Now if you'll excuse me, I have my fiancée to attend to."

"No, it won't work that way, you'll pluck her out of time just before we're all destroyed." I hated it when Brownlow didn't listen to me, like I was some petulant child. I wasn't wrong, and I hadn't been before when his steam-works threatened to set all of London aflame. But, like then, it was no use.

He was set in his ways and too stubborn to be saved. He ignored my pleas and continued about his work. His focus was centered on the central stream of white light as winds whooshed around us and figures flickered in the center of the circle. One of them was Miss Leeford, I was sure. She was coming.

Something else was happening outside of Brownlow's angular perimeter.

My feet.

They were getting wet.

A surge of water puddled around us as if an unexpected tide was coming in. Water seeped through the grass before the grass itself changed into a sandy beach. The ground rumbled, as green gave way to brown and softness turned to coarse hardness.

"What's happening?" Pip asked, cradling Stella's head above the encroaching water.

"It's salty," she said weakly as a small wave splashed into her face.

"The ocean," I called. The ocean had been here since the beginning. Out of everything in Earth's time, the oceans and its life had been here the longest. Whether this was localized to us or whether the waters threatened to swallow the world whole, it was proof that once time stopped, the brief blink that humanity had existed in would be snuffed out like a candle in a storm.

Mr. Brownlow had no idea what his device was doing, the destruction it was truly capable of. He had returned to his work, oblivious to the chaos in the park and all around us.

The sea began to rise. Gone was the sandy beach. The cold water must have brought Dodger back to consciousness because she jumped upright as the dark waters began to engulf her.

"What the bloody hell?" she asked.

"Another time slip." What else could go wrong?

"Oliver there's movement in the water," Pip warned.

I've got to stop asking that.

After eyeing the black water, I saw it too. Dodger trudged over to me and we both splashed over to Stella, watching our steps as short, snake-like creatures slithered around our legs.

The water was now knee high as Pip pulled Stella toward the receding shore. We met them there, as a creature took hold of Pip's leg. With a scream, Pip dipped below the surface. Stella splashed down as we raced to them. Blood bubbled to the surface. Dodger reached Stella and pulled her away as I searched frantically for Pip. My heart stopped beating until he kicked back up a moment later, holding a creature above the water.

"Lampreys," he yelled in disgust. "Keep them off you, they bite hard." It looked like a long, silver rope, with a nightmare mouthful of teeth at one end.

I forced my way to the grassy shore of Hyde Park and out of the water near Stella and Dodger, kicking the floppy lamprey bloodsuckers away. One sliced through my leg as it tried to attach itself like a toothy suction cup, but I managed to pull it off before it clamped on. I took ahold of Pip and pulled him to shore.

Blood ran down my leg and salt water soaked the grass underneath us. Pip sprang to Stella and Dodger stood as a sentinel, on guard for any further surprises.

As we regrouped, I saw that the surge of seawater, about ten feet wide and half as deep, had an unintended effect on Mr. Brownlow's defenses. Weak lightning cracked around the water, fizzling. A series of cracks popped off in rapid succession, followed by a firework display of sparks shooting out.

"His barrier is down," Dodger said.

"If it's down, how's his time-machine still powered?" I asked.

"It doesn't matter. Now's our chance."

"We still don't have any idea how to shut him down."

"Stella isn't going to make it," Pip called. Dodger and I knelt over her. She looked pale and slick, and the scarlet stain had only grown, soaking through Pip's fingers.

"I need a hospital," she shuddered. Her whole body began to slowly tremor. "A modern one. Bleeding me or Mercury won't fix it, you have to get me back home, to my time." She addressed Pip and placed a weak hand on his chin. "I'm sorry, Pip. I wish you and I could have had that conversation over coffee."

"Remember when I pulled you from the rubble?" Pip compressed her wound with both hands. "There was a connection between us. A special moment made all the precious because it was fleeting. It doesn't matter how much you have when it's all gone, covered over by time, all that will have mattered are the connections you had, the people you cared for. And I care about you.

"I had a life on the Moors," Pip continued, "but I turned it all down. That was wrong. So wrong. I've found in you someone to care about, and if I can save you, Stella, then maybe I've done something good."

Stella placed her hands over Pip's, lacing her fingers through his. She said weakly, "It only took all this blood to show me that I do have a heart."

"Oliver," Pip pleaded. "Are you right about this being the end? That we're a flash in time, gone forever if we don't stop him?"

"Yes," I said. "I'm right." Moments were made through love and loss, of birth and death, of living on through others through our own selfish acts. Life was painful, but it was miraculous too. It wasn't your clothes and your house, or your pedigree, it was in the people you chose to spend those brief specks with. If time were to stop, so too would those seconds, those tiny bits of space, where life truly existed.

"So, if Brownlow is wrong and Stella dies, I'll never see her again," Pip thought out loud. "But if we stop him, get her back to her time, then I'll still never see her again?"

"But she'll live," came the muffled voice of Nell. Stella let go of Pip's hands and removed from her pocket the timepiece, our only chance. She placed the pocket watch in my hand. I opened it as Nell continued. "Brownlow's machine is self-sustaining; it's a matter of moments now."

"We have Oliver's watch," Pip smiled. "We can use it, turn back time, win."

"Turn back to when?" Dodger asked. "To put it bluntly, you boys have been losing the entire time. You can't beat Brownlow. But Nell can."

"Dodger's right. It would buy you minutes, but that won't be enough," Nell said. "The only way to finish this is to get me in there and let his unnatural man-made machine fight the supernatural. In other words, Oliver, I'm the only one who has a chance."

"How?" I asked urgently.

"Get me into that ray of light flowing out from his time-machine," Nell's dulcet voice assured. "I can do the rest. I can shut it down and reset everything."

"Ghostbusters." Stella coughed out a stifled laugh. "Cross the streams. Last movie I ever rewatched with my dad."

"Right then," I said. Nell was in control of time. Natural time. She had to have a way. "And everyone goes back to where they came from?"

"Yes," Nell answered sadly. "But there's a cost. I can't get there by myself; whoever takes me, gets me inside that time-stream, may become trapped somewhere, sometime, never to return."

The words hung like the gallows' rope at dawn.

"It's time. It's 8:40. You lose," Brownlow said. "Thank you for allowing me to reach this moment."

Within the beam of light, a ghostly apparition appeared. It was of a soft woman, kind, warm, keen. She was Brownlow's lost fiancée. I felt pity for him in that moment. He had done all of this for her. Part of me wanted to see him succeed, to see him happy. If he was, then maybe I could have a piece of my father back.

But it wasn't worth the price he was willing to pay.

"Darling," Brownlow sobbed, stretching out to her, "I've missed you so much."

"We're out of time," Nell said.

"I know what must be done," I said, listening to my gut. There was no hesitation. Pip had pointed out my problem, that I never knew what to do. But I did now.

"I see what you're doing, Oliver, and I won't let you do it," Pip said. He gave Stella a kiss on her forehead and motioned Dodger over, who took his place by Stella's side while transferring pressure on her wound.

"That's the point, Pip," I explained. "You said I need to start trusting myself. Listening to my instincts. *Trust me.* I know how to beat Brownlow."

"It shouldn't be you."

"You're right," I said, handing him the watch.

Pip's eyes widened but we both knew that this was the right choice. He eyed Stella and nodded at me.

"Thank you," he said. The watch began to glow as he took ahold of it. He charged Brownlow's radiant tower, with one last glance behind him, shouting, "tally-ho!"

Nell charged up whatever powers she had cooking to shut down the time stream. Copper colors swirled from the watch as Pip raced into the darkness ahead. Below Pip's feet, grass sprang back to place and the water disappeared as firm ground reformed. It was as if Nell was turning back the clock just for him, giving Pip both more time and solid earth to storm over. In a flash, he was at the equipment, twisting through a pair of faraday discs.

But he wasn't charging into Brownlow. He was ignoring the tower of light altogether as if in a feint. I squinted my eyes in case I wasn't seeing that right. Sure enough, his path was askew.

"What is he doing?" Dodger's voice was uncertain.

"Trust him," I said coolly. "I think I see what he's doing."

"No matter what you choose," I could hear Mr. Brownlow's self-assured voice, "I told you, Oliver, you can't stop me."

Dodger and I watched as Mr. Brownlow, his back still turned away, confidently stepped blindly over to the right.

Right into Pip's path.

"I'm not Oliver," Pip plowed into the old man. They both tumbled into the time-machine so very close to the bright, white time-stream.

"Pip, you?" Brownlow asked, slack jawed. "How could you? After everything I expected from you."

"Oh, did I twist those expectations?" Pip placed my watch, along with Nell, into the light.

"Please, don't," Brownlow begged. It was too late. The beam brightened at first, but then flickered, like a flame. Red-orange and brownish color snaked up the beam constricting it, pushing it down. The bright lights battled, flashing and streaking in the night sky until Nell's copper colors overpowered Brownlow's machine. His fiancée faded away.

"No!" Brownlow cried out.

The white ray of light flashed out as colors exploded in the sky like fireworks in a deafening blast. Blades of grass blew backwards as a sweeping wind turned into a gale-burst that sent me staggering into Dodger. We braced each other as the shockwave bellowed past.

"It was always supposed to be Twist!" The blast knocked his head into the hard copper pipes of his time-machine. Mr. Brownlow slumped slowly to the ground as Pip and the time-stream disappeared. "I tried to save Helena; I was supposed to save her—"

As the lights went out, the sky cracked and thundered. Fog swirled and swept outward, giving us a view of stars.

As the night air calmed, my watch clattered to the ground, rolled on its side a ways, before rattling to a stop. Dodger and I headed toward it.

The waters receded and disappeared. Stella's unconscious form vanished. Brownlow's time-machine was splintered, bent, and wrecked. Dodger and I approached Brownlow's semi-conscious form as the world returned to normal and moonlight bathed the sky with a blueish glow.

Oddly enough, the Crystal Palace did not return. It remained absent as if it had been an affront to nature itself; the mighty elm stood tall, its branches swaying freely in the open breeze.

Pip was nowhere to be found. Nell was right. He was gone, lost somewhere in time. I wondered where and when he was or if we would ever see him again.

"Did we win?"

Yes, and no. I was sad about Pip. He'd proposed a partnership with The Orphan, but it was Pip that had become the hero. We might have been envious of what each other had at first, but what we'd both come to realize was that there were more important things to life. Like friendship and feelings. I would miss him dearly. All I could muster to Dodger was a bittersweet response. "Something like that."

"What do we do next?"

"A good friend told me that we don't have a lot of time here, that it matters above all else who we spend our lives with. Who we love."

"I never said that I love—"

"Oh, I know," I said, pulling her closer. I kissed her, not wanting to waste another second.

Chapter 30
Loose Threads

The Zulus:

Mandla awaited death.

The Viking Chief was set to oblige as he brandished his axe overhead for the killing blow.

A blast came from afar that blinded the battlefield. The Viking stilled his strike and Mandla's vision blurred. The tall column of copper-colored and white battling lights blinked out; he could tell that much. And a second later, a shockwave shook through them.

The Viking stumbled, wiping his eyes and steadying his stance. The giant beast that stood beside them cocked its head away from the explosion. They were distracted. That was all the opening Mandla needed. He took the broken spear below the blade above the break, and shoved it upward, as he'd taught himself, into the gut of the man who would have slain him.

The Viking Chief gasped; his jaw hung wide. He emitted a gurgle that was soon followed by a thick gush of blood. He stepped back, bumping into the recovering beast . . .

The dinosaur growled, a low, powerful rumble that made Mandla's hands tremble. With one jerk of its giant jaws, the Megalosaurus ripped into the Viking, catching the unsuspecting meal tightly in its mouth. The beast reared its head, picking the man up with his feet flailing skyward. All Mandla heard next was screaming and crunching.

His tribe cheered as the Vikings raised their weapons high above their heads and yelled in reaction to their leader's demise. As the Vikings rushed in, the first, a blond with a dented helm and bloody blade disappeared. They slowed their assault, looking around in confusion, Mandla and the Zulus watched as one by one the Vikings vanished. The beast, with its meal in its mouth, was gone too.

Soon, his tribesmen were disappearing. The Englishmen had been true to their word. The few Zulus that remained, Mandla included, broke into a chant, a hymn of hope and respect to worthy opponents.

We will return home the victors, Mandla thought, as he felt himself being whisked away from this terrible place, *and put our dead to rest, so that they may live on through us.*

***

The Foundlings:

"They're mamas," Abbey said with beaming eyes. The dinosaurs had scared Edward and Byron. But they didn't scare her, not anymore. "You big blokes are blocking their way, let them get back to their babies."

The three of them did so, stepping slowly to the side and away from the nests, through the sharp blackthorns. After they had made it a few feet away, the dinosaurs smoothed their feathers back into a slick sheen. They waggled their tails like puppies and hopped hurriedly to their nests. All except for the smaller dinosaur, who wandered around curiously.

"They must have been separated when they got stuck here." Byron said.

"They weren't trying to attack us," Abbey realized, "They were trying to get back."

"Now that I think about it," Edward explained, "their behavior inside the Palace was strange. Maybe they wanted our help."

Four of the five cooing creatures settled in among the three mounds, with two, possibly a mamma and a papa, settling over their clutch of eggs.

"Oh, they're so sweet." Her attention turned to the one left alone. The fifth little bird-lizard tried to join a nest only to be chased away. It hung its head low. "The baby doesn't have a nest. He doesn't have a family," she pouted.

Suddenly, the white column of light that had been shooting skyward stopped shining. It went out in a blinding flash of darkness that made Abbey shake. A wave, like an invisible hand, pushed her and the others down to the ground. She watched as the dinosaurs braced on their nests, protecting their young.

The small dinosaur rushed toward Abbey, hiding behind her as the scary wave slowed and stopped. She could feel the warmth of the creature pressed against her back and feel it shiver. It was more afraid than she was. "It's okay," Abbey coaxed. "It's okay."

As darkness descended and the air quieted, the small dinosaur came out from behind her back and sat comfortably in Abbey's lap. They watched as the dinosaurs and their nests all went away. All except for one. The baby dinosaur nestled with Abbey made a soft, happy chirp. She petted it, scratching behind its head. The dinosaur pressed its head into her palm, hoping for more.

"Why didn't he go with the others?" Byron asked.

"I don't know." Edward stood, eyeing the scene as the gentle glow of the moon broke free of the fog and shined out over them.

Abbey's mouth twisted into a big smile. "Can we keep him?"

***

Oliver:

"You-" The familiar, if not weak voice, interrupted the tender kiss between Dodger and me. We broke our embrace and faced Mr. Brownlow once more. My heart sank. I thought we were rid of his schemes for—

Brownlow stumbled out from in front of the wreckage of his machine, one hand covering a weltering bruise that oozed redly, and the other hand pointing an accusing finger at me. He looked woozy, faint, as if he was going to fall.

I raced over, covering the few feet of distance at Mercurial speed.

He collapsed wordlessly in my arms. I caught him, but I wasn't prepared for his full weight, it was all I could do to get us both down to the ground as gently as possible.

I waited for him to give me something, anything, a struggle, or a fight, or a last admonition, but he gave me only a wheezing rattle of breath . . .

And nothing more.

I didn't know what that meant, it couldn't be that he was dead, I didn't know what to do, we were on the ground, he was supposed to talk to me, he was my father and now—

He was gone.

And there was nothing I could do as I watched helplessly as he was stolen away.

I didn't even cry. Not then. I don't know why. My first reaction surprised me. It was anger. How could he do this to me? How could he have turned out this way and left me with nothing, no fatherly wisdom, no advice, nothing to explain himself or why he had done the things he'd done? I squeezed my fists as hard as I could. He had made no attempt at reconciliation, no attempt to push past our differences, to at least give me a glimpse of what we had meant to each other so long before.

There was nothing.

***

I closed his eyes.

***

It wasn't fair.

***

I felt a gentle, loving tug at my coat. It was Dodger, who offered me her hand. She pulled me up. "I'm so sorry. I know this must be hard for you."

"Thank you," I whispered. She was there for me to lean on, so I did. That surprised me as well.

Together, we moved and laid Brownlow's body onto his time-machine. It felt appropriate. I found a dusky frock coat rumpled up on his chair and used it to cover him. Inspector Bucket would be along shortly with his Peelers, and we could begin arrangements. Until that time, I didn't want the foundlings seeing him.

I turned back to Dodger, taking her hands. I was appreciative of her presence, as my heart poured out a cornucopia of wild emotions from this long, weary day.

***

Dodger and I, for most of our lives, had been opponents, always sizing each other up, looking for weakness. I suppose we'd found something else. She had gone from saving me on those cold church steps so long ago, to teaching me how to thieve, to outright murdering me in cold blood, to becoming someone I found I could not live without.

I realized why my adopted father had been so determined to be with the woman he loved. It didn't make his actions right, but I found a sort of peace in it that settled my soul.

"Oliver, I need to tell you something," she began to whisper to me, but the apparition appeared again, cloaked in black, knitting away at the threads of time. My blood chilled and my bones ached, and a black pit swallowed my chest whole.

A black void, colored in copper swirls, opened beneath the Dark Spirit. She hovered over it, pointing a knitting needle at me.

"What's wrong?" Dodger asked, before she could finish telling me what I already knew. I wasn't sure if she could see it too.

"Dodger, you have to know—"

A knitting needle shot out from the figure. It came at me like a spear, attached to a wiry black thread of yarn, and pierced my ankle. I let out a yelp at the sudden pain.

My head swam with questions. What was going on? Was this what Nell had warned me about: the cost of her interference, her efforts to save us all? I knew there would be a price, but not this, not now, not when Dodger and I—

"What's going on, what is this?" Dodger asked, pleadingly.

The cloaked figure gave a yank, and I was swept off my feet. The copper-colors circled like a drain hole as I was inexorably pulled into it. I ripped into the ground with my fingers but managed only to claw out clumps of grass.

The figure went through the portal, I reached out for Dodger's hand but it slipped away. My heart raced.

"Dodger," I said, no longer bothering to tell her how I felt but instead trying to tell her, warn her, but the chance was lost as I fell through the hole. "She told me that you—"

***

Dodger:

The night went dark and silent. The copper swirls were gone, as was Oliver. What was he trying to tell her? What the bloody hell had happened? She stared at the patch of green into which Oliver had been pulled a moment ago.

There was one person who might have answers. She'd seen Oliver's watch drop to the ground earlier when Nell had stopped the time-stream. Dodger searched for it and found it among bits of gears and copper pipes from the destroyed time-machine.

She took another moment to stare at it before bending over to scoop it up, as if picking up not a watch, but a burden. It was hers now, her responsibility, at least until she found Ollie, if she could.

"He's gone," the voice of Nell said. "And it's all my fault. I'm sorry, Dodger, I didn't know."

"Where did he go? What do we do now?" Dodger asked as the foundlings raced over. They looked rough around the edges, but they were resilient, hardy kids, and they were alive. For that, Dodger was thankful. But their night was only starting.

"Where's Mr. Twist?" Edward asked, nursing his injured arm. Behind Byron, Abbey looked coolly at the watch, a tear forming in her eye. A small critter chirped and darted around her legs. It looked as if she had rescued a stray pup.

Dodger could only shake her head at Abbey. She was *not* going to keep a dinosaur, but that was a conversation for later. First, they had work to do.

"Oliver could be anywhere," Nell said. "At any point in time. There's no way to know."

"Bloody 'ell my luck." Dodger said, clicking shut the timepiece. "We're going to find Ollie, I promise. And I'm going to punch him."

Epilogue

The brick interior and shelves stacked with pulpy, almond-scented paperbacks in the Book Club Bar outside the NYU campus made him feel a little more at home in this strange, new place. He made the queue through the leisurely line, a familiar routine, until he was utterly lost at the counter.

"I'd like a lah-tay, uhm, please?" he said to the purple-haired barista. It had taken him awhile to gain his bearings and even longer to find the right coffee place. But after a time, he found it. Now, if he could only figure out how to order.

"A latte?" She shot him a goofy grin. She wore a black apron and had a small metal ball attached to her nose. A tattoo of a sea-turtle decorated her arm, which he noticed when she waved to the large menu overheard that listed everything from wines to cocktails and coffee. "What kind of milk, Mr. English?"

"From a cow?"

"Send it, honey," she snorted. "I love that you're keeping character, its right out of *Bridgerton*. Love the accent." She punched buttons into what was likely a till. "Five dollars and seventy-five cents."

He rumbled through his pockets and produced several notes. That was way too much for a coffee, it was half a years' salary for some, but he didn't have any choice. Sheepishly, he handed the bills over, realizing too late that the barista probably couldn't do anything with his outdated currency.

She waved it away. "You aren't the first starving actor to step in here. Tell you what, it's on the owner if you give me something in return. Give me your hand."

He did so. Perhaps this was a custom or some sort of way of handling debt? The purple-haired girl scribbled onto his palm. When she finished, she handed him a hot latte in a paper cup before he could look at what she'd written.

"Good luck with your audition, honey," she said, waving the next customer over. "You'll get it."

He wove through the clusters of tables and chairs, each full of bustling young people busy with their lives. Again, it was not too dissimilar a scene from a busy London pub except for the scandalous manner of dress and glowing rectangular things everyone seemed to hold in front of their faces.

Finally, he came upon her.

She was sitting head down and alone at a table for two, with her books out, and a notebook filled with equations. Her hair was straight, and she wore a claret-colored jacket over a baggy brown sweater which likely hid thick bandages that would have been wrapped around her stomach. She wore trousers – denim and baby blue in color – and they weren't out-of-place here.

"May I sit?" he asked.

"I'm studying, go away." She didn't even look up. "Unless you know calculus."

"I do, in point-of-fact, know about Sir Isaac Newton," he said, placing the coffee down. "Unless maths has changed in the last hundred years or so?"

"Pip?" She looked up as her jaw hit the table. "What are you doing here?"

"It looks like I'm tutoring you, at present."

"No, I mean . . .," Stella's pencil fell and rolled into the spine of the opened textbook. "How?"

"I trusted Twist, I did the thing, and something, or rather someone, must have pulled me here," Pip said, eyeing Stella warmly. "But we must have arrived at separate times. How is your wound?"

"Mending. It's been about a month." She rubbed her stomach and took a short, ragged breath. "No stage recitals for me for awhile."

"I arrived a few hours ago, took me awhile to locate you."

"That long?" Stella took a sip of the latte. "And you buy the first girl you meet a coffee?"

"Second."

"Oh?" Stella sipped the coffee. "This isn't oatmilk."

"I don't know what that is."

"I suppose you wouldn't."

"There's a lot to learn about this place. For starters, can you tell me what this means?" Pip showed Stella his hand.

"It means," Stella took note of the series of numbers scrawled in blue ink as she took his hand. "It means, I'm jealous." She didn't let go. "I wondered what that was like."

"Oh, well, I better call upon her," he said slyly.

"Behave, or I'll punch you in the patriarchy, Pip." Stella closed her books with her free hand. "Sit down."

He took the chair, as his heart pounded against his chest. She took both his hands in hers and they sat in the comforts of the cozy cafe. He thought back to the dark morning mists that had rolled in so long ago on the moors. They had at long last risen out, and in this great new light, he saw in her a shadowless expanse of endless expectations.

Epilogue: Part II

The mud broke my fall.

I squelched around the thick, molasses like muck as I collected my bearings. I must not have fallen far, but searching my surroundings, I saw no trace of copper colors or of the portal I'd been pulled through.

The Spirit of Death was nowhere to be seen, the black-cloaked figure knitting with her needles of fate was gone. Instead, I saw dirty, muddy streets and horse-drawn carriages and styles of frocks, hats, and petticoats on passersby from a bygone generation. They paid no heed to me and my strange, unruffled shirt, and shorter frock coat, as I struggled to discover where and *when* I was.

There were urchins playing in the streets, a wafting presence of manure and horses, and chatter in a silky-spoken language foreign to me. It was both familiar and strange, good and bad. It could have been worse, but I had hoped for better.

My heart sank when, at last, all the clues connected. I was so close to London, but so far. From atop a square stone structure with wooden window frames and white walls, a tricolor flag flapped in the wind.

"Oh, no," I gulped as the realization hit me. I was in France, generations before my time, with no way home.

Oliver Twist returns in *A Twist of Two Cities*

About the Author

Brent A. Harris is a two-time alternate history Sidewise Award finalist. He writes of time-traveling astronaut dinosaurs, misunderstood orcs, conflicted AIs, and a universe where Dickens meets steampunk. You can learn more by visiting www.BrentAHarris.com.

If you've enjoyed this book, please leave a quick review. Reviews matter.

Other books by the author:

A Time of Need: A Dark Eagle Novel
(An alternate history of the American Revolution)

A Twist in Time

A Christmas Twist

Alyx: An AI's Guide to Love and Murder

Twilight of the Mesozoic Moon and other Time-Travel Twists

www.ingramcontent.com/pod-product-compliance
Lightning Source LLC
Chambersburg PA
CBHW051221210726
48290CB00003B/734